Praise for
THE RETRIEVAL ARTIST SERIES

One of the top ten greatest science fiction detectives of all time.

—io9

The SF thriller is alive and well, and today's leading practitioner is Kristine Kathryn Rusch.

—Analog

[Miles Flint is] one of 14 great sci-fi and fantasy detectives who out-Sherlock'd Holmes. [Flint] is a candidate for the title of greatest fictional detective of all time.

—Blastr

If there's any such thing as a sci-fi *CSI*, the Retrieval Artist novels set the tone.

—The Edge Boston

What links [Miles Flint] to his most memorable literary ancestors is his hard-won ability to perceive the complex nature of morality and live with the burden of his own inevitable failure.

—Locus

A nifty series cooks on.

·Booklist

D1603846

Rusch does a superb job of making the Retrieval Artist books work as fully satisfying standalone mysteries and as installments in a gripping saga full of love, loss, grief, hope, adventure, and discovery. It is also some of the best science fiction ever written.

—*New York Times* bestselling author
Orson Scott Card

Readers of police procedurals as well as fans of SF should enjoy this mystery series.

—*Kliatt*

What links [Miles Flint] to his most memorable literary ancestors is his hard-won ability to perceive the complex nature of morality and live with the burden of his own inevitable failure.

—*Locus*

Part CSI, part Blade Runner, and part hard-boiled gumshoe, the retrieval artist of the series title, one Miles Flint, would be as at home on a foggy San Francisco street in the 1940s as he is in the domed lunar colony of Armstrong City.

—*The Edge Boston*

Rusch defines emotional and intellectual cores in her stories and then plots the most fruitful and gorgeously panoramic orbits around them.

—*Wigglefish.com*

Praise for
THE DISAPPEARED

Rusch creates an interesting and fairly original solar civilzation in this new book, apparently the first in a series about Retrieval Artists, a group of specialized agents. It's a balanced blend of police procedural and action adventure....

— Don D'Ammassa
Science Fiction Chronicle

If you've ever enjoyed mysteries, cop novels, hard-boiled detective stories, you're going to be a sucker for *The Disappeared*.

— Lisa DuMond
SF Site

Rusch has created an entertaining blend of mystery and sf, a solid police drama that asks hard questions about what justice between cultures, and even species, really is.

—*Booklist*

It feels like a popular TV series crossed with a Spielberg film—engaging...

—*Locus*

The Retrieval Artist Series:

The RETRIEVAL ARTIST

A RETRIEVAL ARTIST SHORT NOVEL

KRISTINE KATHRYN RUSCH

WMG
Publishing

The Retrieval Artist

Published 2012 by WMG Publishing
www.wmgpublishing.com
First published in *Analog SF*, June, 2000
Cover art copyright © Cammeraydave/Dreamstime
Book and cover design
copyright © 2012 by WMG Publishing
Cover design by Allyson Longueira/WMG Publishing
ISBN-13: 978-0-615-69847-2
ISBN-10: 0-615-69847-6

WMG Publishing
www.wmgpublishing.com

The RETRIEVAL ARTIST

A RETRIEVAL ARTIST SHORT NOVEL

I HAD JUST COME OFF A DIFFICULT CASE, AND THE last thing I wanted was another client. To be honest, not wanting another client is a constant state for me. Miles Flint, the reluctant Retrieval Artist. I work harder than anyone else in the business at discouraging my clients from seeking out the Disappeared. Sometimes the discouragement fails and I get paid a lot of money for putting a lot of lives in danger, and maybe, just maybe, bringing someone home who wants to come. Those are the moments I live for, the moments when it becomes clear to a Disappeared that home is a safe place once more.

Usually though, my clients and their lost ones are more trouble than they're worth. Usually, I won't take their cases for any price, no matter how high.

I do everything I can to prevent client contact from the start. The clients who approach me are the courageous ones or the really desperate ones or the ones who want to use me to further their own ends.

I try not to take my cases personally. My clients and their lost ones depend on my objectivity. But every once in a while, a case slips under my defenses — and never in the way I expect.

This was one of those cases. And it haunts me still.

2

MY OFFICE IS ONE OF THE UGLIEST DIVES ON THE MOON. I found an original building still made of colonial permaplastic in the oldest section of Armstrong, the Moon's oldest colony. The dome here is also made of permaplastic, the clear kind, although time and wear have turned it opaque. Dirt covers the dome near the street level. The filtration system tries to clean as best it can, but ever since some well-meaning dome governor pulled the permaplastic flooring and forgot to replace it, this part of Armstrong Dome has had a dust problem. The filtration systems have been upgraded twice in my lifetime, and rebuilt at least three times since the original settlement, but they still function at one-tenth the level of the state-of-the-art systems in colonies like Gagarin Dome and Glenn Station. Terrans newly off the shuttle rarely come to this part of Armstrong; the high-speed trains don't run here, and the unpaved streets strike most Terrans as unsanitary, which they probably are.

The building that houses my office had been the original retail center of Armstrong, or so says the bronze plaque that someone had attached to the plastic between my door and the rent-a-lawyer's beside me. We are an historic building, not that anyone seems to care, and rent-a-lawyer once talked to me about getting the designation changed so that we could upgrade the facilities.

I didn't tell him that if the designation changed, I would move.

You see, I like the seedy look, the way my door hangs slightly crookedly in its frame. It's deceptive. A careless Tracker would think I'm broke, or equally careless. Most folks don't guess that the security in my little eight-by-eight cube is state of the art. They walk in, and they see permaplastic, and a desk that cants slightly to the right, and only one chair behind it. They don't see the recessed doors that hide my storage in the wall between the rent-a-lawyer's cube and my own, and they don't see the electronics because they aren't looking for them.

I like to keep the office empty. I own an apartment in one of Armstrong's better neighborhoods. There I keep all the things I don't care about. Things I do care about stay in my ship, a customized space yacht named *The Emmeline*. She's my only friend and I treat her like a lover. She's saved my life more times than I care to think about, and for that (and a few other things), she deserves only the best.

I can afford to give her the best, and I don't need any more work although, as I said, I sometimes take it. The cases that catch me are usually the ones that catch me in my Sir Galahad fantasy — the one where I see myself as a rescuer of all things worthy of rescue — although I've been known to take cases for other reasons.

But, as I'd said, I'd just come off a difficult case, and the last thing I needed was another client. Especially one as young and innocent as this one appeared to be.

She showed up at my door wearing a dress, which no one wears in this part of Armstrong any more, and regular shoes, which had to have been painful to walk in. She also had a personal items bag around her wrist, which, in this part of town, was like wearing a giant *Mug Me!* sign. The bags were issued on shuttles and only to passengers who had no idea about the luggage limitations.

She was tall and raw-boned, but slender, as if diet and exercise had reduced her natural tendency toward lushness. Her dress, an open and inexpensive weave, accented her figure in an almost unconscious way. Her features were strong and bold, her eyes dark, and her hair even darker.

My alarm system warned me she was outside, staring at the door or the plaque or both. A small screen popped up on my desk revealing her and the street beyond. I shut off the door alarm, and waited until she knocked. Her clutched fist, adorned with computer and security enhancements that winked like diamonds in the dome's fake daylight, rapped softly on the permaplastic. The daintiness of the movement startled me. I wouldn't have thought her a dainty woman.

I had been cleaning up the final reports, notations and billings from the last case. I closed the file and the keyboard (I never use voice commands for work in my office — too easily overheard) folded itself into the desk. Then I leaned back in the chair, and waited.

She knocked three times, before she tried the door. It opened, just like it had been programmed to do in instances like this.

"Mr. Flint?" Her voice was soft, her English tinted with a faintly Northern European accent.

I still didn't say anything. She had the right building and the right name. I would wait to see if she was the right kind of client.

She squinted at me. I was never what clients expected. They expected a man as seedy as the office, maybe one or two unrepaired scars, a face toughened by a hard life and space travel. Even though I was thirty-five, I still had a look some cultures called angelic: blond curls, blue eyes, a round and cherubic face. A client once told me I looked like the pre-Raphaelite paintings of Cupid. I had smiled at him and said, *Only when I want to.*

"Are you Mr. Flint?" The girl stepped inside, then slapped her left hand over the enhancements on her right. She looked faintly startled, as if someone had shouted in her ear.

Actually, my security system had cut in. Those enhancements linked her to someone or something outside herself, and my system automatically severed such links, even if they had been billed as unseverable.

"You want to stay in here," I said, "you stay in here alone. No recording, no viewing, and no off-site monitoring."

She swallowed, and took another step inside. She was playing at being timid. The real timid ones, severed from their security blankets, bolt.

"What do you want?" I asked.

She flinched, and took another step forward. "I understand that you — find — people."

"Where did you hear that?"

"I was told in New York." One more step and she was standing in front of my desk. She smelled faintly of lavender soap mixed with nervous sweat. She must have come here directly from the shuttle. A woman with a mission, then.

"New York?" I asked as if I'd never heard of it.

"New York City."

I had several contacts in New York, and a handful of former clients. Anyone could have told her, although none were supposed to. They always did though; they always saw their own desperation in another's eyes, figured it was time to help, time to give back whatever it was they felt they had gained.

I sighed. "Close the door."

She licked her lips — the dye on them was either waterproof or permanent — and then walked back to the door. She looked into the street as if she would find help there, then gently pushed the door closed.

I felt a faint hum through my wrist as my computer notified me that it had turned the door security back on.

"What do you want?" I asked before she turned around.

"My mother," she said. "She's —"

"That's enough." I kept my tone harsh, and I didn't stand. I didn't want this girl/woman to be too comfortable. It was always best to keep potential clients off balance.

7

Children, young adults, and the elderly were the obvious choices of someone trying to use my system for the wrong purposes, and yet they were the ones most likely to contact me. They never seemed to understand the hostility I had to show clients, the insistence I put on identity checks, and they always balked at the cost. *It feels as if I'm on trial, Mr. Flint,* they would say, and I wouldn't respond. They were. They had to be. I always had to be sure they were only acting on their own interests. It was too easy for a Tracker to hire someone to play off a Retrieval Artist's sympathies, and initiate a search that would get the Disappeared killed — or worse.

The girl turned. Her body was so rigid that it looked as if I could break her in half.

"I don't find people," I said. "I uncover them. There's a vast difference. If you don't understand that, then you don't belong here."

That line usually caused half my potential clients to exit. The next line usually made most of the remaining fifty percent excuse themselves, never to darken my door again.

"I charge a minimum of two million credits, Moon issue, not Earth issue —" which meant that they were worth triple what she was used to paying — "and I can charge as much as ten million or more. There is no upper limit on my costs nor is there one on my charges. I charge by the day, with expenses added in. Some investigations take a week, some take five years. You would be my exclusive employer for the period of time it takes to find your — mother — or whomever I'd be looking for. I have a contract. Several of my former clients have tried to have the courts nullify it. It holds up beautifully. I do not take charity cases, no matter what your sob story is, and I do not allow anyone to defer payment. The minute the money stops, so do I."

She threaded her fingers together. Her personal items bag bumped against her hip as she did so. "I'd heard about your financial requirements." Which meant that one of my former clients had recommended me to her. Dammit. "I have limited funds, but I can afford a minor investigation."

I stood. "We're done talking. Sorry I can't help you." I walked past her and pulled open the door. Security didn't mind if I did that. It would have minded if she had.

"Can't you do a limited search, Mr. Flint?" Her eyes were wide and brown. If she was twenty, she was older than I thought. I checked for tears. There were none. She could be legit, and for that I was sorry.

I closed the door so hard the plastic office shook. "Here's what you're asking me," I said. "If the money runs out, I quit searching, which is no skin off my nose. But I'll have dug a trail up to that particular point, and your mother — or whomever I'm looking for —"

She flinched again as I said that. A tender one. Or a good actress.

"— would be at more of a risk than she is now. Right now, she's simply disappeared. And since you've come to me, you've done enough research to know that one of six government programs — or one of fifteen private corporations — have gone to considerable expense to give her a new life somewhere else. If the cover on that existence gets blown, your mother dies. It's that simple. And maybe, just maybe, the people who helped her will die too, or the people who are now important to her, or the people who were hidden with her, for whatever reason. Half an investigation is a death sentence. Hell, sometimes a full investigation is a death sentence. So I don't do this work on whim, and I certainly don't do it in a limited fashion. Are we clear?"

She nodded, just once, a rabbit-like movement that let me know I'd connected.

"Good," I said and pulled the door back open. "Now get out."

She scurried past me as if she thought I might physically assault her, and then she hurried down the street. The moon dust rose around her, clinging to her legs and her impractical dress, leaving a trail behind her that was so visible, it looked as if someone were marking her as a future target.

I closed the door, had the security system take her prints and DNA sample off the jamb just in case I needed to identify her someday, and then tried not to think of her again.

It wouldn't be easy. Clients were rare and, if they were legit, they always had an agenda. By the time they found me, they were desperate, and there was still a part of me that was human enough to feel sympathy for that.

Sympathy is rare among Retrieval Artists. Most Retrieval Artists got into this line of work because they owed a favor to the Disty, a group of aliens who'd more or less taken over Mars. Others got into it because they had discovered, by accident, that they were good at it, usually making that discovery in their jobs for human corporations or human crime syndicates.

I got in through a different kind of accident. Once I'd been a space cop assigned to Moon Sector. A lot of the Disappeared come through here on their way to new lives, and over time, I found myself working against a clock, trying to save people I'd never met from the people they were hiding from. The space police frowned on the work — the Disappeared are often reformed criminals and not worth the time, at least according to the Moon Sector — and so, after one of the most horrible incidents of my life, I went into business on my own.

I'm at the top of my profession, rich beyond all measure, and usually content with that. I chose not to have a spouse or children, and my family is long-dead, which I actually consider to be a good thing. Families in this business are a liability. So are close friends. Anyone who can be broken to force you to talk. I don't mind being alone.

But I do hate to be manipulated, and I hate even more to take revenge, mine or anyone else's. I vigilantly protect myself against both of those things.

And this was the first time I failed.

3

After the girl left, I stayed away from the office for two days. Sometimes snubbed clients come back. They tell me their stories, the reasons they're searching for their parent/child/spouse, and they expect me to understand. Sometimes they claim they've found more money. Sometimes they simply try to cry on my shoulder, believing I will sympathize.

Once upon a time maybe I would have. But Sir Galahad has calluses growing on his heart. I am beginning to hate the individuals. They always take a level of judgment that drains me. The lawyers trying to find a long-lost soul to meet the terms of a will; the insurance agents, required by law to find the beneficiaries, forced by the government to search "as far as humanly possible without spending the benefits"; the detective, using government funds to find the one person who could put a career criminal, serial killer, or child molester, away for life; these people are the clients I like the most. Almost all are repeat customers. I still have to do background checks, but I have my gut to rely on as well. With individuals, I can never go by gut, and even armed with information, I've been burned.

I've gotten to the point where coldness is the way of the game for me, at least at first. Once I sign on, I become the most intense defender of the Disappeared. The object of my search also becomes the person I protect and care about the most. It takes a lot of effort to maintain that caring, and even more to manage the protection.

Sometimes I'll go to extremes.

Sometimes I have no other choice.

On the third day, I went back to my office, and of course, the girl was waiting. This time she was dressed appropriately, a pair of boots, cargo pants that cinched at the ankles, and a shirt the color of sand. Her personal items bag was gone — obviously someone, probably the maitre d at the exclusive hotel she was most likely staying at, told her it made her a mark for pickpockets and other thieves. Thin mesh gloves covered her enhancements. Only her long hair marked her as a newcomer. If she stayed longer than a month, she'd cut it off just like the rest of us rather than worry about keeping it clean.

She was leaning against my locked door, her booted feet sticking into the street. In that outfit, she looked strong and healthy, as if she were hiring me to take her on one of those expeditions outside the dome. The rent-a-lawyer next door, newly out of Armstrong Law, was eyeing her out of his scarred plastic window, a sour expression on his thin face. He probably thought she was scaring away business.

I stopped in the middle of the street. It was hot and airless as usual. There was no wind in the dome, of course, and the recycled air got stale real fast. Half the equipment in this part of town had been on the fritz for the last week, and the air here wasn't just stale, it was thin and damn near rancid. I hated breathing bad air. The shallow breaths, and the increased heartbeat made me feel as if there was danger around when there probably wasn't. If the air got any thinner, I'd have to start worrying about my clarity of thought.

She saw me when I was still several meters from the place. She stood, brushed the dust off her pants, and watched me. I pretended as if I were undecided about my next move, even though I knew I'd have to confront her sooner or later. Her kind only went away when chased.

"I'm sorry," she said as I approached. "I was told that you expected negotiation, so I —"

"Lied about the money, did you?" I asked, knowing she was lying now too. If she knew enough to find me, she also knew that I didn't negotiate. All the lie proved was that she had an ego big enough to believe that the rules were different for her.

I shoved past her to use my palm to unlock the door. I only used a palm scan when someone else was present. It let us in, but initiated a higher level of security monitoring.

She started to follow me, but I slammed the door in her face. Then I went to my desk, and switched on my own automatic air. It was illegal, and it wouldn't be enough, but I wasn't planning to stay long. I would finish the reports from the last case, get the final fees, and then maybe I'd take a vacation. I had never taken one before. It was past time.

I wish, now, that I had listened to my gut and gone. But there was just enough of Sir Galahad left in me to make me watch the door. And of course, it opened just like I expected it to.

She came inside, a little downtrodden but not defeated. Her kind seldom were. "My name is Anetka Sobol," she said as if I should know it. I didn't. "I really do need your help."

"You should have thought of that before," I said. "This isn't a game."

"I'm not trying to play one."

"So what was that attempt at negotiation?"

She shook her head. "My source —"

"Who is your source?"

"He said I wasn't —"

"Who is it?"

Again she licked that lower lip just like she had the day before, a movement that was too unconscious to be planned. The nervousness, then, wasn't feigned. "Norris Gonnot."

Gonnot. Sobol was the third client he'd sent to me in the last year. The other two checked out, and both cases had been easy to solve. But he was making himself too visible, and I would have to deal with that, even though I hated to do so. He was extremely grateful that I had found his daughter and granddaughter alive (although they hadn't appreciated it), and he'd been even more grateful when I was able to prove that the Disty were no longer looking for them.

"And how did you find him?"

She frowned. "Does it matter?"

I leaned back in my chair. It squeaked and the sound made her jump ever so slightly. "Either you're up front with me now or the conversation ends."

The frown grew deeper, and she clutched her left wrist with her right hand, holding the whole mess against her stomach. The gesture looked calculated. "Do you treat everyone like this?"

"Nope. Some people I treat worse."

"Then how do you get any work?"

I shrugged. "Just lucky."

She stared at me for a moment. Then she glanced at the door. Was she letting her thoughts be that visible on purpose or was she again acting for my benefit? I wasn't sure.

"A cop told me about him. Norris, that is." She sounded reluctant. "I wasn't supposed to tell you."

"Of course not. Gonnot wasn't supposed to talk to anyone. This cop, was he a rent-a-cop, a real cop, a Federal cop, or with the Earth Force?"

"She," she said.

"Okay," I said. "Was she a —"

"She was a New York City police officer who had her own detective agency."

"That's illegal in New York."

She shrugged. "So?"

I closed my eyes. Ethics had disappeared every-where. "You hired her?"

"She was my fifth private detective. Most would work for a week and then quit when they realized that searching for an interstellar Disappeared is a lot harder than finding a missing person."

I waited. I'd heard that sob story before. Most detectives kept the case and simply came to someone like me.

"Of course," she said, "my father's looming presence doesn't help either."

"Your father?"

She was staring at me as if I had just asked her what God was.

"I'm Anetka Sobol," she said as if that clarified everything.

"And I'm Miles Flint. My name doesn't tell you a damn thing about my father."

"My father is the founding partner of the Third Dynasty."

I had to work to hide my surprise. I knew what the Third Dynasty was, but I didn't know the names of its founders. The Dynasty itself was a formidable presence all over the galaxy. It was a megacorp with its fingers in a lot of pies, mostly to do with space exploration, establishing colonies in mineral rich areas, and exploitation of new resources. My contacts with the Third Dynasty weren't on the exploration level, but within its narrow interior holdings. The Third Dynasty was the parent company for Privacy Unlimited, one of the services which helped people disappear.

Privacy Unlimited had been developed, as so many of the corporate disappearance programs had, when humans discovered the Disty, and realized that in some alien cultures, there was no such word as forgiveness. The Disty were the harshest of our allies. The Revs, the Wygnin, and the Fuetrer also targeted certain humans, and our treaties with these groups allowed the targeting if the aliens could show cause.

The balance was a delicate one, allowing them their cultural traditions while protecting our own. Showing cause had to happen before one of eighteen multicultural tribunals, and if one of those tribunals ruled in the aliens' favor, the humans involved were as good as dead. We looked the other way most of the time. Most of the lives involved were, according to our government, trivial ones. But of course, those people whose lives had been deemed trivial didn't feel that way, and that was when the disappearance services cropped up. If a person disappeared and could not be found, most alien groups kept an outstanding warrant, but stopped searching.

The Disty never did.

And since much of the Third Dynasty's business was conducted in Disty territory, its disappearance service, Privacy Unlimited, had to be one of the best in the galaxy.

Something in my face must have given my knowledge away, because she said, "Now do you understand my problem?"

"Frankly, no," I said. "You're the daughter of the big kahuna. Go to Privacy Unlimited and have them help you. It's usually not too hard to retrace steps."

She shook her head. "My mother didn't go to Privacy Unlimited. She used another service."

"You're sure?"

"Yes." She brushed a hand alongside her head, to move the long hair. "It's my father she's running from."

A domestic situation. I never get involved in those. Too messy and too complicated. Never a clear line. "Then she didn't need a service at all. She probably took a shuttle here, then a transport for parts unknown."

Anetka Sobol crossed her arms. "You don't seem to understand, Mr. Flint. My father could have found her with his own service if she had done something like that. It's simple enough. My detectives should have been able to find her. They can't."

"Let me see if I can understand this," I said. "Are you looking for her or is your father?"

"I am."

"As a front for him?"

Color flooded her face. "No."

"Then why?"

"I want to meet her."

I snorted. "You're going to a lot of expense for a 'hello, how are you.' Aren't you afraid Daddy will find out?"

"I have my own money."

"Really? Money Daddy doesn't know about? Money Daddy doesn't monitor?"

She straightened. "He doesn't monitor me."

I nodded. "That's why the mesh gloves. Fashion statement?"

She glanced at her enhancements. "I got them. They have nothing to do with my father."

My smile was small. "Your father has incredible resources. You don't think he'd do something as simple as hack into your enhancement files. Believe me, one of those pretty baubles is being used to track you, and if my security weren't as good as it is, another would have been monitoring this conversation."

She put her left hand over her right as if covering the enhancements would make me forget them. All it did was remind me that this time, she didn't react when my security shut down her links. This was one smart girl, and one I didn't entirely understand.

"Go home," I said. "Deal with Daddy. If you want family ties, get married, have children, hire someone to play your mother. If you need genetic information or disease history, see your family doctors. I suspect they'll have all the records you need and probably some you don't. If you want Daddy to leave you alone, I'd ask him first before I go to any more expense. He might just do what you want. And if you're trying to make him angry, I'll bet you've gone far enough. You'll probably be hearing from him very soon."

Her eyes narrowed. "You're so sure of yourself, Mr. Flint."

"It's about the only thing I am sure of," I said, and waited for her to leave.

She didn't. She stared at me for a long moment, and in her eyes, I saw a coldness, a hardness I hadn't expected. It was as if she were evaluating me and finding me lacking.

I let her stare. I didn't care what she thought one way or another. I did wish she would get to the point so that I could kick her out of my office.

Finally she sighed and pursed her lips as if she had eaten something sour. She looked around, probably searching for some place to sit down. She didn't find one. I don't like my clients to sit. I don't want them to be comfortable in my presence.

"All right," she said, and her voice was somehow different. Stronger, a little more powerful. I knew the timidity had been an act. "I came to you because you seem to be the only one who can do this job."

My smile was crooked and insincere. "Flattery."

"Truth," she said.

I shook my head. "There are dozens of people who do this job, and most are cheaper." I let my smile grow colder. "They also have chairs in their offices."

"They value their clients," she said.

"Probably at the expense of the people they're searching out."

"Ethics," she said. "That's why I've come here. You're the only one in your profession who seems to have any."

"You have need of ethics?" Somehow I had trouble believing the woman with that powerful voice had need of anyone with ethics. "Or is this simply another attempt at manipulation?"

To my surprise, she smiled. The expression was stunning. It brought life to her eyes, and somehow seemed to make her even taller than she had been a moment before.

"Manipulation got me to you," she said. "Your Mr. Gonnot seems to have a soft spot for people who are missing family."

"Everyone who's missing is a member of a family," I said, but more to the absent Gonnot than to her. I could see how he could be manipulated, and that made it more important than ever to stop him from sending customers my way.

She shrugged at my comment, then she sat on the edge of my desk. I'd never had anyone do that, not in all my years in the business. "I do have need of ethics," she said. "If you breathe a single word of what I'm going to tell you…"

She didn't finish the sentence, on purpose of course, probably figuring that whatever I could imagine would be worse than what she could come up with.

I sighed. This girl — this woman — liked games.

"If you want the sanctity of a confessional," I said, "see a priest. If you want a profession that requires its practitioners to practice confidentiality as a matter of course, see a psychiatrist. I'll keep confidential whatever I deem worthy of confidentiality."

She folded her slender hands on her lap. "You enjoy judging your clients, don't you?"

I stared at her — up at her — which actually put me at a disadvantage. She was good at intimidation skills, even better than she had been as an actress. It made me uncomfortable, but somehow it seemed more logical for the daughter of the man who ran the Third Dynasty.

"I have to," I said. "A lot of lives depend on my judgments."

She shook her head slightly. It was as if my earlier answer stymied her, prevented her from continuing. She had to learn that we would do this on my terms or we wouldn't do it at all.

I waited. I could wait all day if I had to. Most people didn't have that kind of patience no matter what sort of will they had.

She clearly didn't. After a few moments, she brushed her pants, adjusted the flap on one of the pockets, and sighed again. She must have needed me badly.

Finally, she closed her eyes, as if summoning strength. When she opened them, she was looking at me directly. "I am a clone, Mr. Flint."

Whatever I had thought she was going to say, it wasn't that. I worked very hard at keeping the surprise off my face.

"And my father is dying." She paused, as if she were testing me.

I knew the answer, and the problem. When her father died, she couldn't inherit. Clones were barred from familial inheritance by interstellar law. The law had been adapted universally after several cases where clones created by a non-family member and raised far from the original (wealthy) family inherited vast estates. The basis of the inheritance was a shared biology that anyone could create. Rather than letting large fortunes get leached off to whoever was smart enough to steal a hair from a hairbrush and use it to create a copy of a human being, legislators finally decided to create the law. The courts upheld it. It was rigid.

"Your father could change his will," I said, knowing that she had probably broached this with him already.

"It's too late," she said. "He's been ill for a while. The change could easily be disputed in court."

"So you're not an only child?" I had to work to keep from asking if she were an only copy.

"I am the only clone," she said. "My father had me made, and he raised me himself. I am, for all intents and purposes, his daughter."

"Then he should have changed his will long ago."

She waved a hand, as if the very idea were a silly one. And it probably was. A clone had to come from some-where. So either she was the copy of a real child or a copy of the woman she wanted me to find. Perhaps the will was unchanged because the original person was still out there.

"My mother vanished with the real heir," she said.

I waited.

"My father always expected to find them. My sister is the one who inherits."

I hated clone terminology. "Sister" was such an in-accurate term, even though clones saw themselves as twins. They weren't. They weren't raised that way or thought of that way. The Original stood to inherit. The clone before me did not.

"So you, out of the goodness of your heart, are searching for your missing family." I laid the sarcasm on thick. I've handled similar cases before. Where money was involved, people were rarely altruistic.

"No," she said, and her bluntness surprised me. "My father owns 51% of the Third Dynasty. When he dies, it goes into the corporation itself, and can be bought by other shareholders. I am not a shareholder, but I have been raised from birth to run the Dynasty. The idea was that I would share my knowledge with my sister, and that we would run the business together."

This made more sense.

"So I need to find her, Mr. Flint, before the shares go back into the corporation. I need to find her so that I can live the kind of life I was raised to live."

I hated cases like this. She was right. I did judge my clients. And if I found them the least bit suspicious, I didn't take on the case. If I believed that what they would do would jeopardize the Disappeared, I wouldn't take the case either. But if the reason for the disappearance was gone, or if the reason for finding the missing person benefited or did not harm the Disappeared, then I would take the case.

I saw benefit here, in the inheritance, and in the fact that the reason for the disappearance was dying.

"Your father willed his entire fortune to his missing child?"

She nodded.

"Then why isn't he searching for her?"

"He figured she would come back when she heard of his death."

Possible, depending on where she had disappeared to, but not entirely probable. The girl might not even know who she was.

"If I find your mother," I said, "then will your father try to harm her?"

"No," she said. "He couldn't if he wanted to. He's too sick. I can forward the medical records to you."

One more thing to check. And check I would. I guess I was taking this case, no matter how messily she started it. I was intrigued, just enough.

"Your father doesn't have to be healthy enough to act on his own," I said. "With his money, he could hire someone."

"I suppose," she said. "But I control almost all of his business dealings right now. The request would have to go through me."

I still didn't like it, but superficially, it sounded fine. I would, of course, check it out. "Where's your clone mark?"

She frowned at me. It was a rude question, but one I needed the answer to before I started.

She pulled her hair back, revealing a small number eight at the spot where her skull met her neck. The fine hairs had grown away from it, and the damage to the skin had been done at the cellular level. If she tried to have the eight removed, it would grow back.

"What happened to the other seven?" I asked.

She let her hair fall. "Failed."

Failed clones were unusual. Anything unusual in a case like this was suspect.

"My mother," she said, as if she could hear my thoughts, "was pregnant when she disappeared. I was cloned from sloughed cells found in the amnio."

"Hers or the baby's?"

"The baby's. They tested. But they used a lot of cells to find one that worked. It took a while before they got me."

Sounded plausible, but I was no expert. More information to check.

"Your father must have wanted you badly."

She nodded.

"Seems strange that he didn't alter his will for you."

Her shoulders slumped. "He was afraid any changes he made wouldn't have been lawyer-proof. He was convinced I'd lose everything because of lawsuits if he did that."

"So he arranged for you to lose everything on his own."

She shook her head. "He wanted the family together. He wanted me to work with my sister to —"

"So he said."

"So he says." She ran a hand through her hair. "I think he hopes that my sister will cede the company to me. For a percentage, of course."

There it was. The only loophole in the law. A clone could receive an inheritance if it came directly from the person whose genetic material the clone shared, provided that the Original couldn't die under suspicious circumstances. Of course, a living person could, in Anetka's words, "cede" that ownership as well, although it was a bit more difficult.

"You're looking for her for money," I said in my last ditch effort to get out of the case.

"You won't believe love," she said.

She was right. I wouldn't have.

"Besides," she said. "I have my own money. More than enough to keep me comfortable for the rest of my life. Whatever else you may think of my father, he has provided that. I'm searching for her for the corporation. I want to keep it in the family. I want to work it like I was trained. And this seems to be the only way."

It wasn't a very pretty reason, and I'd learned over the years, it was usually the ugly reasons that were the truth. Not, of course, that I could go by gut. I wouldn't.

"My retainer is two million credits," I said. "If you're lucky, that's all this investigation will cost you. I have a contract that I'll send to you or your personal representative, but let me give you the short version verbally."

She nodded.

I continued, reciting, as I always did, the essential terms so that no client could ever say I'd lied to her. "I have the right to terminate at any time for any reason. You may not terminate until the Disappeared is found, or I have concluded that the Disappeared is gone for good. You are legally liable for any lawsuits that arise from any crimes committed by third parties as a result of this investigation. I am not. You will pay me my rate plus expenses whenever I bill you. If your money stops, the investigation stops, but if I find you've been withholding funds to prevent me from digging farther, I am entitled to a minimum of ten million credits. I will begin my investigation by investigating you. Should I decide you are unworthy as a client before I begin searching for the Disappeared, I will refund half of your initial retainer. There's more but those are the salient points. Is all of that clear?"

"Perfectly."

"I'll begin as soon as I get the retainer."

"Give me your numbers and I'll have the money placed in your account immediately."

I handed her my single printed card with my escrow account embedded into it. The account was a front for several other accounts, but she didn't need to know that. Even my money went through channels. Someone who is good at finding the Disappeared is also good at making other things disappear.

"Should you need to reach me in an emergency," I said, "place 673 credits into this account."

"Strange number," she said.

I nodded. The number varied from client to client, a random pattern. Sometimes, past clients sent me their old amounts as a way to contact me about something new. I kept the system clear.

"I'll respond to the depositing computer from wherever I am, as soon as I can. This is not something you should do frivolously nor is it something to be done to check up on me. It's only for an emergency. If you want to track the progress of the investigation, you can wait for my weekly updates."

"And if I have questions?"

"Save them for later."

"What if I think I can help?"

"Leave me mail." I stood. She was watching me, that hard edge in her eyes again. "I've got work to do now. I'll contact you when I'm ready to begin my search."

"How long will this investigation of me take?"

"I have no idea," I said. "It depends on how much you're hiding."

4

CLIENTS NEVER TELL THE TRUTH. NO MATTER HOW much I instruct them to, they never do. It seems to be human nature to lie about something, even it's something small. I had a hunch, given Anetka Sobol's background, she had lied about a lot. The catch was to find out how much of what she had lied about was relevant to the job she had hired me for. Finding out required research.

I do a lot of my research through public accounts, using fake i.d. It is precautionary, particularly in the beginning, because so many cases don't pan out. If a Disappeared still has a Tracker after her, repeated searches from me will be flagged. Searches from public accounts — especially different public accounts — will not. Often the Disappeared are already famous or become famous when they vanish, and are often the subject of anything from vidspec to school reports.

My favorite search site is a bar not too far from my office. I love the place because it serves some of the best food in Armstrong, in some of the largest quantities. The large quantities are required, given the place's name. The Brownie Bar serves the only marijuana in the area, baked into specially marked goods, particularly the aforementioned brownies. Imbibers get the munchies, and proceed to spend hundreds of credits on food. The place turns quite a profit, and it's also comfortable; marijuana users seem to like their creature comforts more than most other recreational drug types.

Recreational drugs are legal on the Moon, as are most things. The first settlers came in search of something they called "freedom from oppression" which usually meant freedom to pursue an alternative lifestyle. Some of those lifestyles have since become illegal or simply died out, but others remain. The only illegal drugs these days, at least in Armstrong, are those that interfere with the free flow of air. Everything from nicotine to opium is legal — as long as its user doesn't smoke it.

The Brownie Bar caters to the casual user as well as the hard-core and, unlike some drug bars, doesn't mind the non-user customer. The interior is large, with several sections. One section, the party wing, favors the bigger groups, the ones who usually arrive in numbers larger than ten, spend hours eating and giggling, and often get quite obnoxiously wacky. In the main section, soft booths with tables shield clients from each other. Usually the people sitting there are couples or groups of four. If one group gets particularly loud, a curtain drops over the open section of the booth, and their riotous laughter fades into nearly nothing.

My section caters to the hard-core, who sometimes stop for a quick fix in the middle of the business day, or who like a brownie before dinner to calm the stress of a hectic afternoon. Many of these people have only one, and continue work while they're sitting at their solitary tables. It's quiet as a church in this section, and many of the patrons are plugged into the free client ports that allow them access to the Net.

The access ports are free, but the information is not. Particular servers charge by the hour in the public areas, but have the benefit of allowing me to troll using the server or the bar's identicodes. I like that; it usually makes my preliminary searches impossible to trace.

That afternoon, I took my usual table in the very back. It's small, made of high grade plastic designed to look like wood — and it fools most people. It never fooled me, partly because I knew the Brownie Bar couldn't afford to import, and partly because I knew they'd never risk something that valuable on a restaurant designed for stoners. I sat cross-legged on the thick pillow on the floor, ordered some turkey stew — made here with real meat — and plugged in.

The screen was tabletop, and had a keyboard so that the user could have complete privacy. I'd heard other patrons complain that using the Brownie Bar's system required them to read, but it was one of the features I liked.

I started with Anetka, and decided to work my way backwards through the Sobol family. I found her quickly enough; her life was well covered by the tabs, which made no mention of her clone status. She was twenty-seven, ten to twelve years older than she looked. She'd apparently had those youthful looks placed in stasis surgically. She'd look girlish until she died.

Another good fact to know. If there was an original, she might not look like Anetka. Not any more.

Anetka had been working in her father's corporation since she was twelve. Her IQ was off the charts — surgically enhanced as well, at least according to most of the vidspec programs — and she breezed through Harvard and then Cambridge. She did postdoc work at the Interstellar Business School in Islamabad, and was out of school by the time she was twenty-five. For the last two years, she'd been on the corporate fast-track, starting in lower management and working her way to the top of the corporate ladder.

She was, according to the latest feeds, her father's main assistant.

So I had already found Possible Lie Number One: She wasn't here for herself. She was, as I had suspected, a front for her father. Not to find the wife, but to find the real heir.

I wasn't sure how I'd feel if that were true. I needed to find out if, indeed, the Original was the one who'd inherit. If she wasn't, I wouldn't take the case. There'd be no point.

But I wasn't ready to make judgments yet. I had a long way to go. I looked up Anetka's father, and discovered that Carson Sobol had never remarried, although he'd been seen with a bevy of beautiful women over the years. All were close to his age. He never dated women younger than he was. Most had their own fortunes, and many their own companies. He spent several years as the companion to an acclaimed Broadway actress, even funding some of her more famous plays. That relationship, like the others, had ended amicably.

Which led to Possible Lie Number Two: a man who terrorized his wife so badly that she had to run away from him also terrorized his later girlfriends. And while a man could keep something like that quiet for a few years, eventually the pattern would become evident. Eventually one of the women would talk.

There was no evidence of terrorizing in the stuff I found. Perhaps the incidences weren't reported. Or perhaps there was nothing to report. I would vote for the latter. It seemed, from the vidspec I'd read, everyone knew that the wife had left him because of his cruelty. My experience with vidspec reporters made me confident that they'd be on the lookout for more proof of Carson Sobol's nasty character. And if they found it, they'd report it.

No one had.

I didn't know if that meant Sobol had learned his lesson when the wife ran off, or perhaps Sobol had learned that mistreatment of women was bad for business. I couldn't believe that a man could terrify everyone into silence. If that were his methodology, there would be a few leaks that were quickly hushed up, and one or two dead bodies floating around, bodies belonging to folks who hadn't listened. Also, there would be rumors, and there were none.

Granted, I was making assumptions on a very small amount of information. Most of the reports I found about Sobol weren't about his family or his love life, but about the Third Dynasty as it expanded in that period to new worlds, places that human businesses had never been before.

The Third Dynasty had been the first to do business with the Fuetrers, the HDs, and the chichers. It opened plants on Korsve, then closed them when it realized that the Wygnin, the dominant life forms on Korsve, did not — and apparently could not — understand the way that humans did business.

I shuddered at the mention of Korsve. If a client approached me because a family member had been taken by the Wygnin, I refused the case. The Wygnin took individuals to pay off debt, and then those individuals became part of a particular Wygnin family. For particularly heinous crimes, the Wygnin took firstborns, but usually, the Wygnin just took babies — from any place in the family structure — at the time of birth, and then raised them. Occasionally they'd take an older child or an adult. Sometimes they'd take an entire group of adults from offending businesses. The adults were subject to mind control, and personality destruction as the Wygnin tried to remake them to fit into Wygnin life.

All of that left me with no good options. Children raised by the Wygnin considered themselves Wygnin and couldn't adapt to human cultures. Adults who were taken by the Wygnin were so broken that they were almost unrecognizable. Humans raised by the Wygnin did not want to return. Adults who were broken always wanted to return, and when they did, they signed a death warrant for their entire family — or worse, doomed an entire new generation to kidnap by the Wygnin.

But Wygnin custom didn't seem relevant here. Despite the plant closings, the Third Dynasty had managed to avoid paying a traditional Wygnin price. Or perhaps someone had paid, down the line, and that information was classified.

There were other possibles in the files. The Third Dynasty seemed to have touched every difficult alien race in the galaxy. The corporation had an entire division set aside for dealing with new cultures. Not that the division was infallible. Sometimes there were unavoidable errors.

Sylvy Sobol's disappearance had been one of those. It had caused all sorts of problems for both Sobol and the Third Dynasty. The vidspecs, tabs, and other media had had a field day when she had disappeared. The news led to problems with some of the alien races, particularly the Altaden. The Altaden valued non-violence above all else, and the accusations of domestic violence at the top levels of the Third Dynasty nearly cost the corporation its Altade holdings.

The thing was, no one expected the disappearance — or the marriage, for that matter. Sylvy Sobol had been a European socialite, better known for her charitable works and her incredible beauty than her interest in business. She belonged to an old family with ties to several still existing monarchies. It was thought that her marriage would be to someone else from the accepted circle.

It had caused quite a scandal when she had chosen Carson Sobol, not only because of his mixed background and uncertain lineage, but also because some of his business practices had taken large fortunes from the countries she was tied to and spent them in space instead.

He was controversial; the marriage was controversial; and it looked like, from the vids I watched, that the two of them had been deeply in love.

I felt a hand on my shoulder. A waitress stood behind me, holding a large ceramic bowl filled with turkey stew. She smiled at me.

"Didn't want to set it on your work."

"It's fine," I said, indicating an empty spot near the screen. She set my utensils down, and then the bowl. The stew smelled rich and fine, black beans and yogurt adding to the aroma. My stomach growled.

The waitress tapped one of the moving images. "I remember that," she said. "I was living in Vienna. The Viennese thought that marriage was an abomination."

I looked up. She was older than I was, without the funds to prevent the natural aging process. Laugh lines crinkled around her eyes, and her lips — unpainted and untouched — were a faint rose. She smiled.

"Guess it turned out that way, huh? The wife running off like that? Leaving that message?"

"Message?" I asked. I hadn't gotten that far.

"I don't remember exactly what it was. Something like 'The long arm of the Third Dynasty is impossible to fight. I am going where you can't find me. Maybe then I'll have the chance to live out my entire life.' I guess he nearly beat her to death." The waitress laughed, a little embarrassed. "In those days I had nothing better to do than study the lives of more interesting people."

"And now?" I asked.

She shrugged. "I figured out that everybody's interesting. I mean, you've got to try. You've got to live. And if you do, you've done something fascinating."

I nodded. People like her were one of the reasons I liked this place.

"You want something to drink?" she asked.

"Bottled water."

"Got it," she said as she left.

By the time she brought my bottled water, I had indeed found the note. It had been sent to all the broadcast media, along with a grainy video, taken from a hidden camera, of one of the most brutal domestic beatings I'd ever seen. The images were sometimes blurred and indistinct, but the actions were clear. The man had beat the woman senseless.

There was no mention of the pregnancy in any of this. There was, however, notification of Anetka's birth six months before her mother had disappeared.

Which led me to Possible Lie Number Three. Anetka had said her mother traveled pregnant. Perhaps she hadn't. Or, more chillingly, someone had altered the record either before or after the clones were brought to term. There had to be an explanation of Anetka in the media or she wouldn't be accepted. If that explanation had been planted before, something else was going on. If it were planted afterwards, Sobol's spokespeople could have simply said that reporters had overlooked her in their rush to other stories.

I checked the other media reports and found the same story. It was time to go beneath those stories and see what else I could find. Then I would confront Anetka about the lies before I began the search for her mother.

5

I contacted her and we met, not at my office, but at her hotel. She was staying in Armstrong's newest district, an addition onto the dome that caused a terrible controversy before it was built. Folks in my section believe the reason for the thinner air is that the new addition has stretched resources. I know they aren't right — with the addition came more air and all the other regulation equipment — but it was one of those arguments that made an emotional kind of sense.

I thought of those arguments, though, as I walked among the new buildings, made from a beige material not even conceived of thirty years before, a material that's supposed to be attractive (it isn't) and more resistant to decay that permaplastic. This entire section of Armstrong smelled new, from the recycled air to the buildings rising around me. They were four stories high and had large windows on the dome side, obviously built with a view in mind.

This part of the dome is self-cleaning and see-through. Dust does not slowly creep up the sides as it does in the other parts of Armstrong. The view is barren and stark, just like the rest of the Moon, but there's a beauty in the starkness that I don't see anywhere else in the universe.

The hotel was another large four story building. Most of its windows were glazed dark, so no one could see in, but the patrons could see out. It was part of a chain whose parent company was, I had learned the day before, the Third Dynasty. Anetka was doing very little to hide her search from her father.

Inside, the lobby was wide, and had an old-fashioned feel. The walls changed images slowly, showing the famous sites from various parts of the galaxy where the hotels were located. I had read before the hotel opened that the constantly changing scenery took eight weeks to repeat an image. I wondered what it was like working in a place where the view shifted constantly, and then decided I didn't want to know.

The lobby furniture was soft and a comforting shade of dove gray. Piano music, equally soft and equally comforting, was piped in from somewhere. Patrons sat in small groups as if they were posing for a brochure. I went up to the main desk and asked for Anetka. The concierge led me to a private conference room down the main hallway.

I expected the room to be monitored. That didn't bother me. At this point, I still had nothing to hide. Anetka did, but this was her company's hotel. She could get the records, shut off the monitors, or have them destroyed. It would all be her choice.

To my surprise, she was waiting for me. She was wearing another dress, a blue diaphanous thing that looked so fragile I wondered how she managed to move from place to place. Her hair was up and pinned, with diamonds glinting from the soft folds. She also had diamonds glued to the ridge beneath her eyebrows, and trailing down her cheeks. The net effect was to accent her strength. Her broad shoulders held the gown as if it were air, and the folds parted to reveal the muscles on her arms and legs. She was like the diamonds she wore; pretty and glittering, but able to cut through all the objects in the room.

"Have you found anything?" she asked without preamble.

I shut the door and helped myself to the carafe of water on the bar against the nearest wall. There was a table in the center of the room — made, it seemed — of real wood, with matching chairs on the side. There was also a workstation, and a one-way mirror with a view of the lobby.

I leaned against the bar, holding my water glass. It was thick and heavy, sturdy like most things on the Moon. "Your father's will has been posted among the Legal Notices on all the nets for the last three years."

She nodded. "It's common for CEOs to do that to allay stockholder fears."

"It's common for CEOs to authorize the release after they've died. Not before."

Her smile was small, almost patronizing. "Smaller corporations, yes. But it's becoming a requirement for major shareholders in megacorps to do this even if they are not dead. Investigate further, Mr. Flint, and you'll see that all of the Third Dynasty's major shareholders have posted their wills."

I had already checked the other shareholders' wills, and found that Anetka was right. I also looked for evidence that Carson Sobol was dead, and found none.

She took my silence to be disbelief. "It's the same with the other megacorps. Personal dealings are no longer private in the galactic business world."

I had known that the changes were taking place. I had known, for example, that middle managers signed loyalty oaths to corporations, sometimes requiring them to forsake family if the corporation had called for it. This, one pundit had said, was the hidden cost of doing business with alien races. You had to be willing to abandon all you knew in the advent of a serious mistake. The upshot of the change was becoming obvious. People to whom family was important were staying away from positions of power in the megacorps.

I said, "You're not going to great lengths to hide this search from your father."

She placed a hand on the wooden chair. She was not wearing gloves, and mingled among the enhancements were more diamonds. "You seem obsessed with my father."

"Your mother disappeared because of him. I'm not going to find her only to have him kill her."

"He wouldn't."

"Says you."

"This is your hesitation?"

"Actually, no," I said. "My hesitation is that, according to all public records, you were born six months before your mother disappeared."

I didn't tell her that I knew all the databases had been tampered with, including the ones about her mother's disappearance. I couldn't tell if the information had been altered to show that the disappearance came later or that the child had been born earlier. The tampering was so old that the original material was lost forever.

"My father wanted me to look like a legitimate child."

"You are a clone. He knew cloning laws."

"But no one else had to know."

"Not even with his will posted?"

"I told you. It's only been posted for the last three years."

"Is that why you're not mentioned?"

She raised her chin. "I received my inheritance before — already," she said. I found the correction interesting. "The agreement between us about my sister is both confidential and binding."

"'All of my worldly possessions shall go to my eldest child,'" I quoted. "That child isn't even listed by name."

"No," she said.

"And he isn't going to change the will for you?"

"The Disty won't do business with clones."

"I didn't know you had business with the Disty," I said.

She shrugged. "The Disty, the Emin, the Revs. You name them, we have business with them. And we have to be careful of some customs."

"Won't the stockholders be suspicious when you don't inherit?"

Her mouth formed a thin line. "That's why I'm hiring you," she said. "You need to find my sister."

I nodded. Then, for the first time in the meeting, I sat down. The chair was softer than I had expected it would be. I put my feet on the nearest chair. She glanced at them as if they were a lower life form.

"In order to search for people," I said, "I need to know who they're running from. If they're running from the Disty, for example, I'll avoid the Martian colonies, because they're overrun with Disty. No one would hide there. It would be impossible. If they were running from the Revs, I would start looking at plastic surgeons and doctors who specialize in genetic alteration because anyone who looks significantly different from the person the Revs have targeted is considered, by the Revs, to be a different being entirely."

She started to say something, but I held up my hand to silence her.

"Human spouses abuse each other," I said. "It seems to be part of the human experience. These days, the abused spouse moves out, and sometimes leaves the city, sometimes the planet, but more often than not stays in the same area. It's unusual to run, to go through a complete identity change, and to start a new life, especially in your parents' income bracket. So tell me, why did your mother really leave?"

Nothing changed in Anetka's expression. It remained so immobile that I knew she was struggling for control.

The hardness that had been so prevalent the day before was gone, banished, it seemed, so that I wouldn't see anything amiss.

"My father has a lot of money," she said.

"So do other people. Their spouses don't disappear."

"He also controls a powerful megacorp with fingers all over the developing worlds. He has access to more information than anyone. He vowed to never let my mother out of his sight. My father believed that marriage vows were sacred, and no matter how much the parties wanted out, they were obligated by their promises to each other and to God to remain." Anetka's tone was flat too. "If she had just moved out, he would have forced her to move back in. If she had moved to the Moon, he would have come after her. If she had moved to some of the planets in the next solar system, he would have come for her. So she had no choice."

"According to your father."

"According to anyone who knew her." Anetka's voice was soft. "You saw the vids."

I nodded.

"That was mild, I guess, for what he did to her."

I leaned back in the chair, lifting the front two legs off the ground. "So how come he didn't treat his other women that way?"

Something passed through her eyes so quickly that I wasn't able to see what the expression was. Suspicion? Fear? I couldn't tell.

"My father never allowed himself to get close to anyone else."

"Not even his Broadway actress?"

She frowned, then said, "Oh, Linda? No. Not even her. They were using each other to throw off the media. She had a more significant relationship with one of the major critics, and she didn't want that to get out."

"What about you?" I asked that last softly. "If he hurt your mother, why didn't he hurt you?"

She put her other hand on the chair as if she were steadying herself. "Who says he didn't?"

And in that flatness of tone, I heard all the complaints I'd ever heard from clones. She had legal protection, of course. She was fully human. But she didn't have familial protection. She wasn't part of any real group. She didn't have defenders, except those she hired herself.

But I didn't believe it, not entirely. She was still lying to me. She was still keeping me slightly off balance. Something was missing, but I couldn't find it. I'd done all the digging I could reasonably do. I had no direction to go except after the missing wife — if I chose to continue working on this case. This was the last point at which I could comfortably extricate myself from the entire mess.

"You're not telling me everything," I said.

Again, the movement with the eyes. So subtle. So quick. I wondered if she had learned to cover up her emotions from her father.

"My father won't harm her," she said. "If you want, I'll even sign a waiver guaranteeing that."

It seemed the perfect solution to a superficial problem. I had a hunch there were other problems lurking below.

"I'll have one sent to you," I said.

"Are you still taking the case?"

"Are you still lying to me?"

She paused, the dress billowing around her in the static-charged air. "I need you to find my sister," she said.

And that much, we both knew to be true.

6

My work is nine-tenths research and one-tenth excitement. Most of the research comes in the beginning, and it's dry to most people, although I still find the research fascinating. It's also idiosyncratic and part of the secret behind my reputation. I usually don't describe how I do the research — and I never explain it to clients. I usually summarize it, like this:

It took me four months to do the preliminary research on Sylvy Sobol. I started from the premise that she was pregnant with a single girl child. A pregnant woman did one of three things: she carried the baby to term, she miscarried, or she aborted. After dealing with hospital records for what seemed like weeks, I determined that she carried the baby to term. Or at least, she hadn't gotten rid of it before she disappeared.

A pregnant woman had fewer relocation options than a non-pregnant one. She couldn't travel as far or on many forms of transport because it might harm the fetus. Several planets, hospitable to humans after they'd acclimatized, were not places someone in the middle of pregnancy was allowed to go. The pregnancy actually made my job easier, and I was glad for it.

Whoever had hidden her was good, but no disappearance service was perfect. They all had cracks in their systems, some revealing themselves in certain types of disappearance, others in all cases past a certain layer of complexity. I knew those flaws as well as I knew the scars and blemishes on my own hands. And I exploited them with ease.

At the end of four months, I had five leads on the former Mrs. Sobol. At the end of five months, I had eliminated two of those leads. At the end of six months, I had a pretty good idea which of the remaining three leads was the woman I was looking for.

I got in my ship, and headed for Mars.

7

IN THE HUNDRED YEARS SINCE THE DISTY FIRST entered this solar system, they have taken over Mars. The human-run mineral operations and the ship bases are still there, but the colonies are all Disty run, and some are Disty built.

The Emmeline has clearance on most planets where humans make their homes. Mars is no difference. I docked at the Dunes, above the Arctic Circle, and wished I were going elsewhere. It was the Martian winter, and here, in the largest field of sand dunes in the solar system, that meant several months of unrelenting dark.

I had never understood how the locals put up with this. But I hadn't understood a lot of things. The domes here, mostly of human construction, had an artificial lighting system built in, but the Disty hated the approximation of a twenty-four hour day. Since the Disty had taken over the northern most colonies, darkness outside and artificial lights inside were the hallmarks of winter.

The Disty made other alterations as well. The Disty were small creatures with large heads, large eyes, and narrow bodies. They hated the feeling of wide open spaces, and so in many parts of the Sahara Dome, as Terrans called this place, false ceilings had been built in, and corridors had been compressed. Buildings were added into the wider spaces, getting rid of many passageways and making the entire place seem like a rat's warren. Most adult humans had to crouch to walk comfortably through the city streets and some, in disgust, had bought small carts so that they could ride. The result was a congestion that I found claustrophobic at the best of times. I hated crouching when I walked, and I hated the stink of so many beings in such a confined space.

Many Terran buildings rose higher than the ceiling level of the street, but to discourage that wide-open spaces feel, the Disty built more structures, many of them so close together that there was barely enough room for a human to stick his arm between them. Doors lined the crowded streets, and the only identifying marks on most places were carved into the frame along the door's side. The carvings were difficult to see in the weird lighting, even if there weren't the usual crowds struggling to get through the streets to God knew where.

My candidate lived in a building owned by the Disty. It took me two passes to find the building's number, and another to realize that I had found the right place. A small sign, in English, advertised accommodations fit for humans, and my back and I hoped that the sign was right.

It was. The entire building had been designed with humans in mind. The Disty had proven themselves to be able interstellar traders, and quite willing to adapt to local customs when it suited them. It showed in the interior design of this place. Once I stepped through the door, I was able to stand upright, although the top of my head did brush the ceiling. To my left, a sign pointed toward the main office, another pointed to some cramped stairs, and a third pointed to the recreation area.

I glanced at the main office before I explored any farther. The office was up front, and had the same human-sized ceilings. In order to cope, the Disty running the place sat on its desk, its long feet pressed together in concentration. I passed it, and went to the recreation area. I would look for the woman here before I went door to door upstairs.

The recreation area was about half the size of a human-made room for the same purpose. Still, the Disty managed to cram a lot of stuff in here, and the closeness of everything — while comfortable for the Disty — made it uncomfortable for any human. All five humans in the room were huddled near the bar on the far end. It was the only place with a walking path large enough to allow a full-grown man through.

To get there, I had to go past the ping-pong table, and a small section set aside for Go players. Several Disty were playing Go — they felt it was the best thing they had discovered on the planet Earth, with ping-pong a close second — sitting on the tables so that their heads were as near the ceiling as they could get. Two more

Disty were standing on the table, playing ping-pong. None of them paid me any attention at all.

I wound my way through the tight space between the Go players and the ping-pong table, ducking once to avoid being whapped in the head with an out-of-control ping-pong ball. I noted three other Disty watching the games with rapt interest. The humans, on the other hand, had their backs to the rest of the room. They were sitting on the tilting bar stools, drinking, and not looking too happy about anything.

A woman who could have been anywhere from thirty to seventy-five sat at one end of the bar. Her black hair fell to the middle of her back, and she wore make-up, an affectation that the Disty seemed to like. She was slender — anyone who wanted to live comfortably here had to be — and she wore a silver beaded dress that accented that slimness. Her legs were smooth, and did not bear any marks from mining or other harsh work.

"Susan Wilcox?" I asked as I put my hand on her shoulder and showed her my license.

I felt the tension run through her body, followed by several shivers, but her face gave no sign that anything was wrong.

"Want to go talk?"

She smiled at me, a smooth professional smile that made me feel a little more comfortable. "Sure."

She stood, took my hand as if we'd been friends a long time, and led me onto a little patio someone had cobbled together in a tiny space behind the recreation area. I didn't see the point of the thing until I looked up. This was one of the few places in Sahara where the dome was visible, and through its clear surface, you could see the sky. She pulled over a chair, and I grabbed one as well.

"How did you find me?" she asked.

"I'm not sure I did." I held out my hand. In it was one of my palmtop. "I want to do a DNA check."

She raised her chin slightly. "That's not legal."

"I could get a court order."

She looked at me. A court order would ruin any protection she had, no matter who — or what — she was running from.

"I'm not going to see who you are. I want to see if you're who I'm looking for. I have comparison DNA."

"You're lying," she said softly.

"Maybe," I said. "If I am, you're in trouble either way."

She knew I was right. She could either take her chances with me, or face the court order where she had no chance at all.

She extended her hand. I ran the edge of the computer along her palm, removing skin cells. The comparison program ran, and as I turned the palmtop face-up, I saw that there was no match. The only thing this woman shared in common with the former Mrs. Sobol was that they were both females of a similar age, and that they had both disappeared twenty-nine years ago while pregnant. Almost everything else was different.

I used my wrist-top for a double-check, and then I sighed. She was watching me closely, her dark eyes reflecting the light from inside.

I smiled at her. "You're in the clear," I said. "But if it was this easy for me to find you, chances are that it'll be as easy for someone else. You might want to move on."

She shook her head once, as if the very idea were repugnant.

"Your child might appreciate it," I said.

She looked at me as if I had struck her. "She's not who —"

"No," I said. "She's safe. From me at least. And maybe from whoever's after you. But you've survived out here nearly thirty years. You know the value of caution."

She swallowed, hard. "You know a lot about me."

"Not really." I stood. "I only know what you have in common with the woman I'm looking for." I slipped the palmtop into my pocket and bowed slightly. "I appreciate your time."

Then I went back inside, slipped through the recreation area, walked past two more Disty in the foyer, and headed into the narrow passageway they called a street. There I shuddered. I hated the Disty. I'd worked so many cases in which people ran to avoid being caught by the Disty that I'd become averse to them myself.

At least, that was my explanation for my shudder. But I knew that it wasn't a real explanation. I had put a woman's life in jeopardy, and we both knew it. I hoped no one had been paying attention. But I was probably wrong. The only solace I had was that since she was hiding amongst the Disty, she probably wasn't being sought by one of them. If she had been pursued by a Disty, my actions probably would have signed her death warrant.

I spent a night in a cramped hotel room since the Disty didn't allow take-offs within thirty-six hours of landing. And then I got the hell away from Sahara Dome — and Mars.

8

MY SECOND POSSIBILITY WAS IN NEW ORLEANS, which made my task a lot easier. I had former clients there who felt they owed me, some of whom were in related businesses. I had one of those clients break into the Disappeared's apartment, remove a strand of hair, and give it to another former client. A third brought me the strand in my room in the International Space Station. Because the strand proved not to be a match, and because I was so certain it would be, I repeated the procedure once more, this time getting another old friend to remove another hair strand from the suspect's person. Apparently, he passed her in a public place, and plucked. The strand matched the first one, but didn't belong to Sylvy Sobol.

I didn't warn this woman at all because I didn't feel as if I had put her in danger. If she were suspicious about the hair pulling incident, I felt it was her responsibility to leave town on her own.

The third candidate was on the Moon, in Hadley. I had no trouble finding her, which seemed odd, but she didn't check out either. I returned to Armstrong, both stumped and annoyed.

The logical conclusion was that my DNA sample was false — that it wasn't the sample for Sylvy Sobol. I had taken the sample from the Interstellar DNA database, and there was the possibility that the sample had been changed or tainted. I had heard of such a thing being done, but had always dismissed it as impossible. Those samples were the most heavily guarded in the universe. Even if someone managed to get into the system, they would encounter back-ups upon back-ups, and more encryption than I wanted to think about.

So I contacted Anetka and asked her to send me a DNA sample of her mother. She did, and I ran it against the sample I had. Mine had been accurate. The women I had seen were not Sylvy Sobol.

I had never, in my entire career, made an error of this magnitude. One of those women should have been the former Mrs. Sobol. Unless my information was wrong. Unless I was operating from incorrect assumptions. Still, the assumptions shouldn't have mattered in this search. A pregnant woman wasn't that difficult to hide, not when she was taking transport elsewhere. I'd even found the one who'd remained on Earth.

No. The incorrect assumption had to come after the pregnancy ended. The children. Transport registries always keep track of the sex of the fetus, partly as a response to a series of lawsuits where no one could prove that the woman who claimed she'd lost a fetus on board a transport had actually been pregnant. The transports do not do a DNA check — such things are considered violations of privacy in all but criminal matters — but they do require pregnant women to submit a doctor's report on the health of the mother and the fetus before the woman is allowed to board.

I'd searched out pregnant women, but only those carrying a single daughter. Not twins or multiples. And no males.

Anetka had mentioned failed clones. Clones failed for a variety of reasons, but they only failed in large numbers when someone was using a defective gene or was trying to make a significant change on the genetic level. If the changes didn't work at the genetic level, surgery was performed later to achieve the same result and the DNA remained the same.

I had Anetka's DNA. I'd taken it that first day without her knowing it. I ran client DNA only when I felt I had no other choice; sometimes to check identity, sometimes to check for past crimes. I hadn't run Anetka's — photographic, vid, and those enhancements made it obvious that she was who she said she was. I knew she wasn't concealing her identity, and there was no way she was fronting for a Disty or any other race. She had told me she was a clone. So I felt a DNA check was not only redundant, it was also unnecessary because it didn't give me the kind of information I was searching for.

But now things were different. I needed to check it to see if she was a repaired child, if there had been some flaw in the fetus that couldn't have been altered in the womb. I hadn't looked for repaired children when I'd done the hospital records scans. I hadn't looked for anything that complicated at all.

So I ran the DNA scan. It only took a second, and the results were not what I expected.

Anetka Sobol wasn't a repaired child, at least not in the sense that I had been looking for. Anetka Sobol was an altered child.

According to her DNA, Anetka Sobol had once been male.

9

IF THE TRAIL HADN'T BEEN SO EASY TO FOLLOW ONCE I realized I was looking for a woman pregnant with a boy, I wouldn't have traced it. I would have gone immediately to Anetka and called her on it. But the trail was easy to follow, and any one of my competitors would have done so — perhaps earlier because they had different methods than I did. I knew at least three of them that ran DNA scans on clients as a matter of course.

If Anetka went to any of them after I refused to complete the work, they would find her mother. It would take them three days. It took me less, but that was because I was better.

10

Sylvy Sobol ran a small private university in the Gagarin Dome on the Moon. She went by the name Celia Walker, and she had transferred from a school out past the Disty homeworld where she had spent the first ten years of her exile. She had run the university for fifteen years.

Gagarin had been established fifty years after Armstrong, and was run by a governing board, the only colony that had such a government. The board placed covenants on any person who owned or rented property within the interior of the dome. The covenants covered everything from the important, such as oxygen regulators, to the unimportant, such as a maintenance schedule for each building, whether the place needed work or not. Gagarin did not tolerate any rules violations. If someone committed three such violations — whether they be failing to follow the maintenance schedule or murder — that person was banned from the dome for life.

The end result was that residents of Gagarin were quiet, law-abiding, and suspicious. They watched me as if I were a particularly distasteful bug when I got off the high speed train from Armstrong. I learned later that I didn't meet the dome's strict dress code.

I had changed into something more appropriate after I got my hotel room, and then went to the campus. The university was a technical school for undergraduates, most of them local, but a few came in from other parts of the Moon. The administrative offices were in a low building with fake adobe facades. The classrooms were in some of Gagarin's only high rises, and were off limits to visitors.

I didn't care about that. I went straight to the Chancellor's office, and buzzed myself in, even though I didn't have an appointment. Apparently, the open campus policy that the on-line brochures proudly proclaimed extended to the administrative offices as well.

Sylvy Sobol sat behind a desk made of Moon clay. Ancient southwestern tapestries covered the walls, and matching rugs covered the floor. The permaplastic here had been covered with more fake adobe, and the net effect was to make this seem like the American Southwest hundreds of years before.

She looked no different than the age-enhancement programs on my computer led me to believe she'd look. Her dark hair was laced with silver, her eyes had laugh lines in the corners, and she was as slender as she had been when she disappeared. She wore a blouse made of the same weave as the tapestries, and a pair of tan cargo pants. Beneath the right sleeve of her blouse a stylish wrist-top glistened. When she saw me, she smiled. "May I help you?"

I closed the door, walked to her desk, and showed her my license. Her eyes widened ever so slightly, and then she covered the look.

"I came to warn you," I said.

"Warn me?" She straightened almost imperceptibly, but managed to look perplexed. Behind the tightness of her lips, I sensed fear.

"You and your son need to use a new service, and disappear again. It's not safe for you anymore."

"I'm sorry, Mr. — Flint? — but I'm not following you."

"I can repeat what I said, or we can go somewhere where you'd feel more comfortable talking."

She shook her head once, then stood. "I'm not sure I know what we'd be talking about."

I reached out my hand. I had my palm scanner in it. Anyone who'd traveled a lot, anyone who had been on the run, would recognize it. "We can do this the old-fashioned way, Mrs. Sobol, or you can listen to me."

She sat down slowly. Her lower lip trembled. She didn't object to my use of her real name. "If you're what your identification says you are, you don't warn people. You take them in."

I let my hand drop. "I was hired by Anetka Sobol," I said. "She wanted me to find you. She claimed that she wanted to share her inheritance with her Original. She's a clone. The record supports this claim."

"So, you want to take us back." Her voice was calm, but her eyes weren't. I watched her hands. They remained on the desktop, flat, and she was without enhancement. So far, she hadn't signaled anyone for help.

"Normally, I would have taken you back. But when I discovered that Anetka's Original was male, I got confused."

Sylvy licked her lower lip, just like her cloned daughter did. A hereditary nervous trait.

I rested one leg on the corner of the desk. "Why would a man change the sex of a clone when the sex didn't matter? Especially if all he wanted was the child. A man with no violent tendencies, who stood accused of attacking his wife so savagely all she could do was leave him, all she could do was disappear. Why would he do that?"

She hadn't moved. She was watching me closely. Beads of perspiration had formed on her upper lip.

"So I went back through the records and found two curious things. You disappeared just after his business on Korsve failed. And once you moved to Gagarin, you and your son were often in other domed Moon colonies at the same time as your husband. Not a good way to hide from someone, now is it, Mrs. Sobol?"

She didn't respond.

I picked up a clay pot. It was small and very, very old. It was clearly an original, not a Moon-made copy. "And then there's the fact that your husband never bothered to change his will to favor the child he had raised. It wouldn't have mattered to most parents that the child was a clone, especially when the Original was long gone. He could have arranged a dispensation, and then made certain that the business remained in family hands." I set the pot down. "But he had already done that, hadn't he? He hoped that the Wygnin would forget."

She made a soft sound in the back of her throat, and backed away from me, clutching at her wrist. I reached across the desk and grabbed her left arm, keeping her hand away from her wrist-top. I wasn't ready for her to order someone to come in here. I still needed to talk to her alone.

"I'm not going to turn you in to the Wygnin," I said. "I'm not going to let anyone know where you are. But if you don't listen to me, someone else will find you, and soon."

She stared at me, the color high in her cheeks. Her arm was rigid beneath my hand.

"The will was your husband's only mistake," I said. "The Wygnin never forget. They targeted your firstborn, didn't they? The plants on Korsve didn't open and close without a fuss. Something else happened. The Wygnin only target firstborns for a crime that can't be undone."

She shook her arm free of me. She rubbed the spot where my hand had touched her flesh, then she sighed. She seemed to know I wouldn't go away. When she spoke, her voice was soft. "No Wygnin were on the site planning committee. We bought the land, and built the plants according to our customs. At that point, the Wygnin didn't understand the concept of land purchase."

I noted the use of the word "we." She had been involved with the Third Dynasty, more involved than the records said.

"We built on a haven for nestlings. You understand nestlings?"

"I thought they were a food source."

She shook her head. "They're more than that. They're part of Wygnin society in a way we didn't understand. They become food only after they die. It's the shells that are eaten, not the nestlings themselves. The nestlings themselves are considered sentient."

I felt myself grow cold. "How many were killed?"

She shrugged. "The entire patch. No one knows for sure. We were told, when the Wygnin came to us, that they were letting us off easily by taking our firstborn — Carson's and mine. They could easily take all the children of anyone who was connected with the project, but they didn't."

They could have too. It was the Third Dynasty that acted without regard to local custom, which made it liable to local laws. Over the years, no interstellar court had overturned a ruling in instances like that.

"Carson agreed to it," she said. "He agreed so no one else would suffer. Then we got me out."

"And no one came looking for you until I did."

"That's right," she said.

"I don't think Anetka's going to stop," I said. "I suspect she wants her father to change the will —"

"What?" Sylvy clenched her collar with her right hand, revealing the wrist-top. It was one of the most sophisticated I'd seen.

"Anetka wants control of the Third Dynasty, and I was wondering why her father hadn't done a will favoring her. Now I know. She was probably hoping I couldn't find you so that her father would change the will in her favor."

"He can't," Sylvy said.

"I'm sure he might consider it, if your son's life is at stake," I said. "The Wygnin treat their captives like family — indeed, make them into family, but the techniques they use on adults of other species are —"

"No," she said. "It's too late for Carson to change his will."

She was frowning at me as if I didn't understand anything. And it took me a moment to realize how I'd been used.

Anetka Sobol had tricked me in more ways than I cared to think about. I wasn't half as good as I thought I was. I felt the beginnings of an anger I didn't need. I suppressed it. "He's dead, isn't he?"

Sylvy nodded. "He died three years ago. He installed a personal alarm that notified me the moment his heart stopped. My son has been voting his shares through a proxy program my husband set up during one of his trips here."

I glanced at the wrist-top. No wonder it was so sophisticated. Too sophisticated for a simple administrator. Carson Sobol had given it to her, and through it, had notified her of his death. Had it broken her heart? I couldn't tell, not from three years distance.

She caught me staring at it, and brought her arm down. I turned away, taking a deep breath as the reality of my situation hit me. Anetka Sobol had out-maneuvered me. She had put me in precisely the kind of case I never wanted.

I was working for the Tracker. I was leading a Disappeared to her death and probably the death of her son.

"I don't get it," I said. "If something happens to your son, Anetka still won't inherit."

Sylvy's smile was small. "She inherits by default. My son will disappear, and stop voting the proxy program. She'll set up a new proxy program and continue to vote the shares. I'm sure the Board thinks she's the person behind the votes anyway. No one knows about our son."

"Except for you, and me, and the Wygnin." I closed my eyes. "Anetka had no idea you'd had a son."

"No one did," Sylvy said. "Until now."

I rubbed my nose with my thumb and forefinger. Anetka was good. She had discovered that I was the best and the quickest Retrieval Artist in the business. She had studied me and had known how to reach me. She had also known how to play at being an innocent, how to use my past history to her advantage. She hired me to find her Original, and once I did, she planned to get rid of him. It would have been easy for her too; no hit man, no attempt at killing. She wouldn't have had to do anything except somehow — surreptitiously — let the Wygnin know how to find the Original. They would have taken him in payment for the Third Dynasty's crimes, he would have stopped voting his shares, and she would have controlled the corporation.

Stopping Anetka wasn't going to be easy. Even if I refused to report, even if Sylvy and her son returned to hiding, Anetka would continue looking for them.

I had doomed them. If I left this case now, I ensured that one of my colleagues would take it. They would find

Sylvy and her son. My colleagues weren't as good as I was, but they were good. And they were smart enough to follow the bits of my trail that I couldn't erase.

The only solution was to get rid of Anetka. I couldn't kill her. But I could think of one other way to stop her.

I opened my eyes. "If I could get Anetka out of the business, and allow you and your son to return home, would you do so?"

Sylvy shook her head. "This is my home," she said. She glanced at the fake adobe walls, the southwestern decor. Her fingers touched a blanket hanging on the wall beside her. "But I can't answer for my son."

"If he doesn't do anything, he'll be running for the rest of his life."

She nodded. "I still can't answer for him. He's an adult now. He makes his own choices."

As we all did.

"Think about it," I said, handing her a card with my chip on it. "I'll be here for two days."

11

THEY HIRED ME, OF COURSE. WHAT THINKING PERSON wouldn't? I had to guarantee that I wouldn't kill Anetka when I got her out of the business — and I did that, by assuring Sylvy that I wasn't now nor would I ever be an assassin — and I had to guarantee that I would get the Wygnin off her son's trail.

I agreed to both conditions, and for the first time in years, I did something other than tracking a Disappeared.

Through channels, I let it drop that I was searching for the real heir to Carson Sobol's considerable fortune. Then I showed some of my actual research — into the daughter's history, the falsified birth date, the inaccurate records. I managed to dump information about Anetka's cloning and her sex change, and I tampered with the records to show that her clone mark had been faked just as her sex had. Alterations, done at birth, made her look like a clone when she really wasn't.

I made sure that my own work on-line looked like sloppy detecting, but I hid the changes I made in other files. I did all of this quickly and thoroughly, and by the time I was done, it appeared as though Carson Sobol had hidden his own heir — originally a son — by making him into a daughter and passing him off as a clone.

At that point, I could have sat back and let events move forward by themselves. But I didn't. This had become personal.

I had to see Anetka one last time.

I set an appointment to hand deliver my final bill.

12

THIS TIME SHE WAS WEARING EMERALDS, AN ENTIRE sheath covered with them. I had heard that there would be a gala event honoring one of the galaxy's leaders, but I had forgotten that the event would be held in Armstrong, at one of the poshest restaurants on the Moon.

She was sweeping up her long hair, letting it fall just below the mark on the back of her head, when I entered. As she turned, she stabbed an emerald hair comb into the bun at the base of her neck.

"I don't have much time," she said.

"I know." I closed the door. "I wanted give you my final bill."

"You found my sister?" There was a barely concealed excitement in her voice.

"No." The room smelled of an illegal perfume. I was surprised no one had confiscated it when she got off the shuttle and then I realized she probably hadn't taken a shuttle. Even the personal items bag she wore that first day had been part of her act. "I'm resigning."

She shook her head slightly. "I might have known you would. You have enough money now, so you're going to quit."

"I have enough information now to know you're not the kind of person I relish working for."

She raised her eyebrows. The movement dislodged the tiny emerald attached to her left cheek. She caught it just before it fell to the floor. "I thought you were done investigating me."

"Your father's dead," I said. "He has been for three years, although the Third Dynasty has managed to keep that information secret, knowing the effect his death would have had on galactic confidence in the business."

She stared at me for a moment, clearly surprised. "Only five of us knew that."

"Six," I said.

"You found my mother." She stuck the emerald in its spot.

"You found the alarm. You knew she'd been notified of your father's death."

The emerald wasn't staying on her cheek. Anetka let out a puff of air, then set the entire kit down. "I really didn't appreciate the proxy program," she said. "It notified me of my insignificance an hour after my father breathed his last. It told me to go about my life with my own fortune and abandon my place in the Third Dynasty to my Original."

"Which you didn't do."

"Why should I? I knew more about the business than she ever would."

"Including the Wygnin."

She leaned against the dressing table. "You're much better than I thought."

"And you're a lot more devious than I gave you credit for."

She smiled and tapped her left cheek. "It's the face. Youth still fools."

Perhaps it did. I usually didn't fall for it, though. I couldn't believe I had this time. I had simply thought I was being as cautious as usual. What Anetka Sobol had taught me was that being as cautious as usual wasn't cautious enough.

"Pay me, and I'll get out of here," I said.

"You've found my mother. You may as well tell me where she is."

"So you can turn your Original over to the Wygnin?"

That flat look came back into her eyes. "I wouldn't do that."

"How would you prevent it? The Wygnin have a valid debt."

"It's twenty-seven years old."

"The Wygnin hold onto markers for generations." I paused, then added, "As you well know."

"You can't prove what I do and do not know."

I nodded. "True enough. Information is always tricky. It's so easy to tamper with."

Her eyes narrowed. She was smart, probably one of the smartest people I'd ever come up against. She knew I was referring to something besides our discussion.

"So I'm getting out." I handed her a paper copy of the bill — rare, unnecessary, and expensive. She knew that as well as I did. Then, as soon as she took the paper from my hand, I pressed my wrist-top to send the electronic version. "You owe me money. I expect payment within the hour."

She crumpled the bill. "You'll get it."

"Good." I pulled open the door.

"You know," she said, just loud enough for me to hear, "if you can find my mother, anyone can."

"I've already thought of that," I said, and left.

13

THE WYGNIN CAME FOR HER LATER THAT NIGHT, toward the end of the gala. Security tried to stop them until they showed a valid warrant for the heir of Carson Sobol. The entire transaction caused an interstellar incident, and the vidnets were filled with it for days. The Third Dynasty used its attorneys to try to prove that Anetka was the eighth clone, just as everyone thought she was, but the Wygnin didn't believe it.

The beautiful thing about a clone is that it is a human being. It's simply one whose heritage matches another person's exactly, and whose facts of birth are odder than most. These are facts, yes, but they are facts that can be explained in other ways. The Wygnin simply chose to believe my explanations, not Anetka's. It was the sex change that did it. The Wygnin believed that anyone who would change a child's sex to protect it would also brand it with a clone mark, even if the mark wasn't accurate.

Over time, the lawyers lost all of their appeals, and Anetka disappeared into the Wygnin culture, never to be heard from again.

Oh, of course, the Third Dynasty still believes it's being run by Anetka Sobol voting her shares, as she always has, through a proxy program. Her Original apparently decided not to return to claim his prize. He acts as he always planned to, secretly. Only Sylvy Sobol, her son, and I know the person voting those shares isn't Anetka.

After Anetka's future was sealed, I stopped paying attention to the business of the Third Dynasty. I still don't look. I don't want to know if I have traded one monster for another. Some cold-heartedness is trained — and I can make myself think that Carson Sobol never once treated young Anetka with love, affection, or anything bordering civility — but I am smart enough to know that most cold-heartedness is bred into the genes. Just because Anetka is gone, doesn't mean the Original won't act the same way in similar circumstances.

And what is my excuse for my cold-heartedness? I'd like to say I've never done anything like this before, but I have — always in the name of my client, or a Disappeared. This time, though, this time, I did it for me.

Anetka Sobol had out-thought me, had compromised me, and had made me do the kind of work I'd vowed I'd never do. I let a front use me to open a door that would allow other Trackers to find a Disappeared.

People disappear because they want to. They disappear to escape a bad life, or a mistake they've made, or they disappear to save themselves from a horrible death. A person who has disappeared never wants to be found.

I always ignored that simple fact, thinking I knew better. But one man is never a good judge of another, even if he thinks he is.

I tell myself Anetka Sobol would have destroyed her Original if she had had the chance. I tell myself Anetka Sobol was greedy and self-centered. I tell myself Anetka Sobol deserved her fate.

But I can't ignore the fact that when I learned that Anetka Sobol had used me, this case became personal, in a way I would never have expected. Maybe, just maybe, I might have found a different solution, if she hadn't angered me so.

And now she haunts me in the middle of the night. She wakes me out of many a sound sleep. She keeps me restless and questioning. Because I didn't go after her for who she was or what she was planning. I had worked with people far worse than she was. I had met others who had done horrible things, things that made me wonder if they were even human. Anetka Sobol wasn't in their league.

No. I had gone after her for what she had done to me. For what she had made me see about myself. And because I hadn't liked my reflection in the mirror she held up, I destroyed her.

I can't get her back. No one comes back intact from the Wygnin. She will spend the rest of her days there. And I will spend the rest of mine thinking about her.

Some would say that is justice. But I have come to realize, in a universe as complex as this one, justice no longer exists.

If you liked *The Retrieval Artist*,
following is a sample of the award-winning
first novel in the series by Kristine Kathryn Rusch.

The**DISAPPEARED**
A RETRIEVAL ARTIST NOVEL

1

SHE HAD TO LEAVE EVERYTHING BEHIND.

Ekaterina Maakestad stood in the bedroom of her Queen Anne home, the ancient Victorian houses of San Francisco's oldest section visible through her vintage windows, and clutched her hands together. She had made the bed that morning as if nothing were wrong. The quilt, folded at the bottom, waiting for someone to pull it up for warmth, had been made by her great-great-grandmother, a woman she dimly remembered. The rocking chair in the corner had rocked generations of Maakestads. Her mother had called it the nursing chair because so many women had sat in it, nursing their babies.

Ekaterina would never get the chance to do that. She had no idea what would happen to it, or to all the heirloom jewelry in the downstairs safe, or to the photographs, taken so long ago they were collectors items to most people but to her represented family, people she was connected to through blood, common features, and passionate dreams.

She was the last of the Maakestad line. No siblings or cousins to take all of this. Her parents were long gone, and so were her grandparents. When she set up this house, after she had gotten back from Revnata, the human colony in Rev territory, she had planned to raise her own children here.

Downstairs, a door opened and she froze, waiting for House to announce the presence of a guest. But House wouldn't. She had shut off the security system, just as she had been instructed to do.

She twisted the engagement ring on her left hand, the antique diamond winking in the artificial light. She was supposed to take the ring off, but she couldn't bring herself to do so. She would wait until the very last minute, then hand the ring over. If she left it behind, everyone would know she had left voluntarily.

"Kat?" Simon. He wasn't supposed to be here.

She swallowed hard, feeling a lump in her throat.

"Kat, you okay? The system's off."

"I know." Her voice sounded normal. Amazing she could do that, given the way her heart pounded and her breath came in shallow gasps.

She had to get him out of here and quickly. He couldn't be here when they arrived, or he would lose everything too.

The stairs creaked. He was coming up to see her.

"I'll be right down!" she called. She didn't want him to come upstairs, didn't want to see him here one last time.

With her right hand, she smoothed her blond hair. Then she squared her shoulders and put on her courtroom face. She'd been distracted and busy in front of Simon before. He might think that was what was happening now.

She left the bedroom and started down the stairs, making herself breathe evenly. For the last week, she hadn't seen him—pleading work, then making up travel, and a difficult court case. She had been trying to avoid this moment all along.

As she reached the first landing, the stairs curved, and she could see him, standing in the entry. Simon wasn't a handsome man. He didn't use enhancements—didn't like them on himself or anyone. As a result, his hair was thinning on top, and he was pudgy despite the exercise he got.

But his face had laugh lines. Instead of cosmetic good looks, Simon had an appealing rumpled quality, like an old favorite old shirt or a quilt that had rested on the edge of the bed for more than a hundred years.

He smiled at her, his dark eyes twinkling. "I've missed you."

Her breath caught, but she made herself smile back. "I've missed you too."

He was holding flowers, a large bouquet of purple lilacs, their scent rising up to greet her.

"I was just going to leave this," he said. "I figured as busy as you were, you might appreciate something pretty to come home to."

He had House's security combination, just like she had his. They had exchanged the codes three months ago, the same night they got engaged. She could still remember the feelings she had that night. The hope, the possibility. The sense that she actually had a future.

"They're wonderful," she said.

He waited for her to get to the bottom of the stairs, then he handed her the bouquet. Beneath the greenery, her hands found a cool vase, a bubble chip embedded in the glass keeping the water's temperature constant.

She buried her face in the flowers, glad for the momentary camouflage. She had no idea when she would see flowers again.

"Thank you," she said, her voice trembling. She turned away, made herself put the flowers on the table she kept beneath the gilt-edged mirror in her entry.

Simon slipped his hands around her waist. "You all right?"

She wanted to lean against him, to tell him the truth, to let him share all of this—the fears, the uncertainty. But she didn't dare. He couldn't know anything.

"I'm tired," she said, and she wasn't lying. She hadn't slept in the past eight days.

"Big case?"

She nodded. "Difficult one."

"Let me know when you're able to talk about it."

She could see his familiar face in the mirror beside her strained one. Even when she tried to look normal, she couldn't. The bags beneath her eyes hadn't been there a month ago. Neither had the worry lines beside her mouth.

He watched her watch herself, and she could tell from the set of his jaw, the slight crease on his forehead, that he was seeing more than he should have been.

"This case is tearing you apart," he said softly.

"Some cases do that."

"I don't like it."

She nodded and turned in his arms, trying to memorize the feel of him, the comfort he gave her, comfort that would soon be gone. "I have to meet a client," she said.

"I'll take you."

"No." She made herself smile again, wondering if the expression looked as fake as it felt. "I need a little time alone before I go, to regroup."

He caressed her cheek with the back of his hand, then kissed her. She lingered a moment too long, caught between the urge to cling and the necessity of pushing him away.

"I love you," she said as she ended the kiss.

"I love you too." He smiled. "There's a spa down in the L.A. basin. It's supposed to be the absolute best. I'll take you there when this is all over."

"Sounds good," she said, making no promises. She couldn't bear to make another false promise.

He still didn't move away. She resisted the urge to look at the two-hundred-year-old clock that sat on the living room mantel.

"Kat," he said. "You need time away. Maybe we could meet after you see your client and—"

"No," she said. "Early court date."

He stepped back from her and she realized she sounded abrupt. But he had to leave. She had to get him out and quickly.

"I'm sorry, Simon," she said. "But I really need the time—"

"I know." His smile was small. She had stung him, and hadn't meant to. "Call me?"

"As soon as I can."

He nodded, then headed for the door. "Turn your system back on."

"I will," she said as he pulled the door open. Fog had rolled in from the Bay, leaving the air chill. "Thank you for the flowers."

"They were supposed to brighten the day," he said, raising his hands toward the grayness.

"They have." She watched as he walked down the sidewalk toward his aircar, hovering the regulation half foot above the pavement. No flying vehicles were allowed in Nob Hill because they would destroy the view, the impression that the past was here, so close that it would take very little effort to touch it.

She closed the door before he got into his car, so that she wouldn't have to watch him drive away. Her hand lingered over the security system. One command, and it would be on again. She would be safe within her own home.

If only it were that simple.

The scent of the lilacs overpowered her. She stepped away from the door and stopped in front of the mirror again. Just her reflected there now. Her and a bouquet of flowers she wouldn't get to enjoy, a bouquet she would never forget.

She twisted her engagement ring. It had always been loose. Even though she meant to have it fitted, she never did. Perhaps she had known, deep down, that this day would come. Perhaps she'd felt, ever since she'd come to Earth, that she'd been living on borrowed time.

The ring slipped off easily. She stared at it for a moment, at the promises it held, promises it would never keep, and then she dropped it into the vase. Someone would find it. Not right away, but soon enough that it wouldn't get lost.

Maybe Simon would be able to sell it, get his money back. Or maybe he would keep it as a tangible memory of what had been, the way she kept her family heirlooms.

She winced.

Something scuffled outside the door—the sound of a foot against the stone stoop, a familiar sound, one she would never hear again.

Her heart leaped, hoping it was Simon, even though she knew it wasn't. As the brass doorknob turned, she reached into the bouquet and pulled some petals off the nearest lilac plume. She shoved them in her pocket, hoping they would dry the way petals did when pressed into a book.

Then the door opened and a man she had never seen before stepped inside. He was over six feet tall, broad-shouldered and muscular. His skin was a chocolate brown, his eyes slightly flat, the way eyes got when they'd been enhanced too many times.

"Is it true," he said, just like he was supposed to, "that this house survived the 1906 earthquake?"

"No." She paused, wishing she could stop there, wishing she could say no to all of this. But she continued, using the coded phrase she had invented for just this moment. "The house was built the year after."

He nodded. "You're awfully close to the door."

"A friend stopped by."

Somehow, the expression in his eyes grew flatter. "Is the friend gone?"

"Yes," she said, hoping it was true.

The man studied her, as if he could tell if she were lying just by staring at her. Then he touched the back of his hand. Until that moment, she hadn't seen the chips dotting his skin like freckles—they matched so perfectly.

"Back door," he said, and she knew he was using his link to speak to someone outside.

He took her hand. His fingers were rough, callused. Simon's hands had no calluses at all.

"Is everything in its place?" the man asked.

She nodded.

"Anyone expecting you tonight?"

"No," she said.

"Good." He tugged her through her own kitchen, past the fresh groceries she had purchased just that morning, past the half-empty coffee cup she'd left on the table.

The back door was open. She shook her hand free and stepped out. The fog was thicker than it had been when Simon left, and colder too. She couldn't see the vehicle waiting in the alley. She couldn't even see the alley. She was taking her first steps on a journey that would make her one of the Disappeared, and she could not see where she was going.

How appropriate. Because she had no idea how or where she was going to end up.

* * *

JAMAL SAMPLED THE SPAGHETTI SAUCE. The reconstituted beef gave it a chemical taste. He added some crushed red pepper, then tried another spoonful, and sighed. The beef was still the dominant flavor.

He set the spoon on the spoon rest and wiped his hands on a towel. The tiny kitchen smelled of garlic and tomato sauce. He'd set the table with the china Dylani had brought from Earth and their two precious wine glasses.

Not that they had anything to celebrate tonight. They hadn't had anything to celebrate for a long time. No real highs, no real lows.

Jamal liked it that way—the consistency of everyday routine. Sometimes he broke the routine by setting the table with wineglasses, and sometimes he let the routine govern them. He didn't want any more change.

There had been enough change in his life.

Dylani came out of their bedroom, her bare feet leaving tiny prints on the baked mud floor. The house was Moon adobe, made from Moon dust plastered over a permaplastic frame. Cheap, but all they could afford.

Dylani's hair was pulled away from her narrow face, her pale gray eyes red-rimmed, like they always were when she got off of work. Her fingertips were stained black from her work on the dome. No matter how much she scrubbed, they no longer came clean.

"He's sleeping," she said, and she sounded disappointed. Their son, Ennis, was usually asleep when she got home from work. Jamal planned it that way—he liked a bit of time alone with his wife. Besides, she needed time to decompress before she settled into her evening ritual.

She was one of the dome engineers. Although the position sounded important, it wasn't. She was still entry level, coping with clogs in the filtration systems and damage outsiders did near the high-speed train station.

If she wanted to advance, she would have to wait years. Engineers didn't retire in Gagarin Dome, nor did they move to other Moon colonies. In other colonies, the domes were treated like streets or government buildings—something to be maintained, not something to be enhanced. But Gagarin's governing board believed the dome was a priority, so engineers were always working on the cutting edge of dome technology, rather than rebuilding an outdated system.

"How was he?" Dylani walked to the stove and sniffed the sauce. Spaghetti was one of her favorite meals. One day, Jamal would cook it for her properly, with fresh ingredients. One day, when they could afford it.

"The usual," Jamal said, placing the bread he'd bought in the center of the table. The glasses would hold bottled water, but it was dear enough to be wine—they would enjoy the water no less.

Dylani gave him a fond smile. "The usual isn't a good enough answer. I want to hear everything he did today. Every smile, every frown. If I can't stay home with him, I at least want to hear about him."

Ever since they found out Dylani was pregnant, Ennis had become the center of their world—and the heart of Jamal's nightmares. He was smothering the boy and he knew it. Ennis was ten months now—the age when a child learned to speak and walk—and he was beginning to understand that he was a person in his own right.

Jamal had read the parenting literature. He knew he should encourage the boy's individuality. But he didn't want to. He wanted Ennis beside him always, in his sight, in his care.

Dylani understood Jamal's attitude, but sometimes he could feel her disapproval. She had been tolerant of his paranoia—amazingly tolerant considering she had no idea as to the root cause of it. She thought his paranoia stemmed from first-child jitters, instead of a real worry for Ennis's safety.

Jamal wasn't sure what he would do when Ennis had to go to school. In Gagarin, home schooling was not an option. Children had to learn to interact with others—

the governing board had made that law almost a hundred years ago, and despite all the challenges to it, the law still stood.

Someday Jamal would have to trust his boy to others—and he wasn't sure he could do it.

"So?" Dylani asked.

Jamal smiled. "He's trying to teach Mr. Biscuit to fly."

Mr. Biscuit was Ennis's stuffed dog. Dylani's parents had sent the dog as a present from Earth. They also sent some children's vids—flats because Dylani believed Ennis was too young to understand the difference between holographic performers and real people.

Ennis's favorite vid was about a little boy who learned how to fly.

"How's Mr. Biscuit taking this?" Dylani asked.

"I'm not sure," Jamal said. "He's not damaged yet, but a few more encounters with the wall might change that."

Dylani chuckled.

The boiling pot beeped. The noodles were done. Jamal put the pot in the sink, pressed the drain button, and the water poured out of the pot's bottom into the recycler.

"Hungry?" he asked.

She nodded.

"Long day?"

"Two breakdowns in dome security." She grabbed a plate and brought it to the sink. "Every available person worked on repairs."

Jamal felt a shiver run down his back. "I've never heard of that."

"It happens," she said. "Sometimes the jobs are so big—"

"No," he said. "The breakdown in security."

She gave him a tolerant smile. "I usually don't mention it. The dome doors go off-line a lot, particularly near the space port. I think it has something to do with the commands issued by the high-speed trains coming in from the north, but no one will listen to me. I'm too junior. Maybe in my off time…"

But Jamal stopped listening. Another shiver ran down his back. It wasn't Dylani's news that was making him uneasy. The kitchen was actually cold and it shouldn't have been. Cooking in such a small space usually made the temperature rise, not lower.

He went to the kitchen door. Closed and latched.

"…would result in a promotion," Dylani was saying. Then she frowned. "Jamal?"

"Keep talking," he said.

But she didn't. Her lips became a thin line. He recognized the look. She hated it when he did this, thought his paranoia was reaching new heights.

Maybe it was. He always felt stupid after moments like this, when he realized that Ennis was safe in his bed and nothing was wrong.

But that didn't stop him from prowling through the house, searching for the source of the chill. He'd never forgive himself if something happened and he didn't check.

"Jamal."

He could hear the annoyance in Dylani's voice, but he ignored it, walking past her into the narrow hallway between the kitchen and the living room. He turned right, toward their bedroom.

It was dark like Dylani had left it, but there was a light at the very end of the hall. In Ennis's room.

Jamal never left a light on in Ennis's room. The boy napped in the dark. Studies had shown that children who slept with lights on became nearsighted, and Jamal wanted his son to have perfect vision.

"Jamal?"

He was running down the hallway now. He couldn't have slowed down if he tried. Dylani might have left the light on, but he doubted it. She and Jamal had discussed the nightlight issue just like they had discussed most things concerning Ennis.

They never left his window open—that was Dylani's choice. She knew how contaminated the air had become inside the dome, and she felt their environmental filter was better than the government's. No open window, no cooler temperatures.

And no light.

He slid into Ennis's room, the pounding of his feet loud enough to wake the baby. Dylani was running after him.

"Jamal!"

The room looked normal, bathed in the quiet light of the lamp he had placed above the changing table. The crib nestled against one corner, the playpen against another. The changing table under the always closed window—which was closed, even now.

But the air was cooler, just like the air outside the house was cooler. Since Ennis was born, they'd spent extra money on heat just to make sure the baby was comfortable. Protected. Safe.

Jamal stopped in front of the crib. He didn't have to look. He could already feel the difference in the room. Someone else had been here, and not long ago. Someone else had been here, and Ennis was not here, not any longer.

Still, he peered down at the mattress where he had placed his son not an hour ago. Ennis's favorite blanket was thrown back, revealing the imprint of his small body. The scents of baby powder and baby sweat mingled into something familiar, something lost.

Mr. Biscuit perched against the crib's corner, his thread eyes empty. The fur on his paw was matted and wet where Ennis had sucked on it, probably as he had fallen asleep. The pacifier that he had yet to grow out of was on the floor, covered in dirt.

"Jamal?" Dylani's voice was soft.

Jamal couldn't turn to her. He couldn't face her. All he could see was the gold bracelet that rested on Ennis's blanket. The bracelet Jamal hadn't seen for a decade. The symbol of his so-called brilliance, a reward for a job well done. He had been so proud of it when he received it, that first night on Korsve. And so happy to leave it behind two years later.

"Oh, my God," Dylani said from the door. "Where is he?"

"I don't know." Jamal's voice shook. He was lying. He tried not to lie to Dylani. Did she know that his voice shook when he lied?

As she came into the room, he snatched the bracelet and hid it in his fist.

"Who would do this?" she asked. She was amazingly calm, given what was happening. But Dylani never panicked. Panicking was his job. "Who would take our baby?"

Jamal slipped the bracelet into his pocket, then put his arms around his wife.

"We need help," she said.

"I know." But he already knew it was hopeless. There was nothing anyone could do.

* * *

THE HOLOVID PLAYED AT ONE-TENTH NORMAL SIZE in the corner of the space yacht. The actors paced, the sixteenth-century palace looking out of place against the green-and-blue plush chairs beside it. Much as Sara loved this scene—Hamlet's speech to the players—she couldn't concentrate on it. She regretted ordering up Shakespeare. It felt like part of the life she was leaving behind.

Sara wondered if the other two felt as unsettled as she did. But she didn't ask. She didn't really want the answers. The others were in this because of her, and they rarely complained about it. Of course, they didn't have a lot of choice.

She glanced at them. Ruth had flattened her seat into a cot. She was asleep on her back, hands folded on her stomach like a corpse, her curly black hair covering the pillow like a shroud.

Isaac stared at the holovid, but Sara could tell he wasn't really watching it. He bent at his midsection, elbows resting on his thighs, his care-lined features impassive. He'd been like this since they left New Orleans, focused, concentrated, frozen.

The yacht bounced.

Sara stopped the holovid. Space yachts didn't bounce. There was nothing for them to bounce on.

"What the hell was that?" she asked.

Neither Ruth nor Isaac answered. Ruth was still asleep. Isaac hadn't moved.

She got up and pulled up the shade on the nearest portal. Earth mocked her, blue and green viewed through a haze of white. As she stared at her former home, a small oval-shaped ship floated past, so close it nearly brushed against the yacht. Through a tiny portal on the ship's side, she caught a glimpse of a human face. A white circle was stamped beneath the portal. She had seen that symbol before: it was etched lightly on the wall inside the luxurious bathroom off the main cabin.

Her breath caught in her throat. She hit the intercom near the window. "Hey," she said to the cockpit. "What's going on?"

No one answered her. When she took her finger off the intercom, she didn't even hear static.

She shoved Isaac's shoulder. He glared at her.

"I think we're in trouble," she said.

"No kidding."

"I mean it."

She got up and walked through the narrow corridor toward the pilot's quarters and cockpit. The door separating the main area from the crew quarters was large and thick, with a sign that flashed *No Entry without Authorization*.

This time, she hit the emergency button, which should have brought one of the crew into the back. But the intercom didn't come on and no one moved.

She tried the door, but it was sealed on the other side.

The yacht rocked and dipped. Sara slid toward the wall, slammed into it, and sank to the floor. Seatbelt lights went on all over the cabin.

Ruth had fallen as well. She sat on the floor, rubbing her eyes. Isaac was the only one who stayed in his seat.

The yacht had stabilized.

"What's going on?" Ruth asked.

"That's what I'd like to know," Sara said.

She grabbed one of the metal rungs, placed there for zero-g flight, and tried the door again. It didn't open.

"Isaac," she said, "can you override this thing?"

"Names," he cautioned.

She made a rude noise. "As if it matters."

"It matters. They said it mattered from the moment we left Earth—"

The yacht shook, and Sara smelled something sharp, almost like smoke, but more peppery.

"Isaac," she said again.

He grabbed the rungs and walked toward her, his feet slipping on the tilted floor. Ruth pulled herself into her chair, her face pale, eyes huge. Sara had only seen her look like that once before—when they'd seen Ilanas's body in the newsvids, sprawled across the floor of their rented apartment in the French Quarter.

Isaac had reached Sara's side. He was tinkering with the control panel beside the door. "Cheap-ass stuff," he said. "You'd think on a luxury cruiser, they'd have up-to-date security."

The door clicked and Isaac pushed it open.

Sweat ran down Sara's back, even though the yacht hadn't changed temperature. The smell had grown worse, and there was a pounding coming from the emergency exit just inside the door.

Isaac bit his lower lip.

"Hello?" Sara called. Her voice didn't echo, but she could feel the emptiness around her. There was no one in the galley, and the security guard who was supposed to be sitting near the cockpit wasn't there.

Isaac stayed by the emergency exit. He was studying that control panel. Ruth had crawled across her cot, and was staring out the panel on her side of the ship. Her hands were shaking.

Sara turned her back on them. She went inside the cockpit—and froze.

It was empty. Red lights blinked on the control panels. The ship was on autopilot, and both of its escape pods had been launched. A red line had formed on a diagram of the ship, the line covering the emergency exit where the noise had come from. More red illuminated the back of the ship.

She punched vocal controls. They had been shut off—which explained why silence had greeted her when she tried the intercom, when she hit the emergency switch, even when she had touched the sealed door.

Warning, the ship's computer said. *Engines disabled. Breach in airlock one. Intruder alert.*

Sara sat in the pilot's chair. It had been years since she'd tried to fly a ship and she'd never operated anything this sophisticated. She had to focus.

Warning.

First she had to bring the controls back online. Most of them had been shut off from the inside. She didn't want to think about what that meant. Not now.

Intruder alert.

She needed visuals. She opened the ports around her, and then wished she hadn't.

A large white ship hovered just outside her view, its pitted hull and cone-shaped configuration sending a chill through her heart.

The Disty had found her—and they were about to break in.

To continue reading this book for free, go to https://www.smashwords.com/books/view/41106 and enter coupon code CW25U.

ABOUT THE AUTHOR

International bestselling writer Kristine Kathryn Rusch has won or been nominated for every major award in the science fiction field. She has won Hugos for editing *The Magazine of Fantasy & Science Fiction* and for her short fiction. She has also won the *Asimov's Science Fiction Magazine* Readers Choice Award six times, as well as the Anlab Award from *Analog Magazine*, *Science Fiction Age* Readers Choice Award, the Locus Award, and the John W. Campbell Award. Her standalone sf novel, *Alien Influences*, was a finalist for the prestigious Arthur C. Clarke Award. *Io9* said her Retrieval Artist series featured one of the top ten science fiction detectives ever written. She writes a second sf series, the Diving Universe series, as well as a fantasy series called The Fey. She also writes mystery, romance and fantasy novels, occasionally using the pen names Kris DeLake, Kristine Grayson and Kris Nelscott.

The Retrieval Artist Series:

wMg
Publishing

21732789R00073

Made in the USA
Lexington, KY
26 March 2013